HIS WORST NIGHTMARE

HIS WORST

NIGHTMARE

BY

TRACY WILSON

Published by
Beautiful Publications LLC
Stratford, CT 06614

LIBRARY OF CONGRESS CONTROL NUMBER: 2024902786

PRINT ISBN: 979-8-9891003-5-4
EBOOK ISBN: 979-8-9891003-4-7

Printed in the United States of America

Content Warning

"This story includes references to domestic violence, suicide, and abortion."

Table of Contents

Content Warning..ix

PROLOGUE 1

1 3

2 13

3 19

4 26

5 33

6 41

7 48

8 57

9 70

10 78

11 84

12 90

13 100

14 109

15 117

16 127

17 136

18 144

19 155

20 162

21 172

22 181

23 189

24 198

25 206

26 215

27 223

28 233

29 242

30 253

31 263

EPILOGUE 272

DISCUSSION 279

NOTE FROM THE AUTHOR 281

PROLOGUE

I was blindsided. He made me love him. He gave me everything I wanted. He was great in bed. He was attentive to all my needs. He was a great father. His son, Billy, was so adorable. He latched onto me and wrapped his fingers around my heart. His mother, Dawn, was so nice it was eerie. I questioned it at first, but they had a dream for sale of us all being one big happy family. They led me to believe that we could all co-parent in harmony and I bought it. She even offered to be the photographer and videographer at our wedding after he surprised me with a proposal in front of his friends where she was also the photographer and videographer. I didn't see anything wrong with any of this. I accepted his proposal, we got married, and I moved into their house. She didn't live there anymore but she came over every day to help their son with his homework.

At first, I was under the delusion that we were happily co-parenting but once the fog dissipated, I began to realize how toxic this marriage was.

"*I* can't wait to get upstairs and get out of these clothes..." I sighed as I closed the door...

"Hi Mommy..." Billy greeted...

"Hi Baby..." I greeted as I headed upstairs... "Oh Hell No!" I gritted as I heard laughter coming from our bedroom... "Get Out!" I demanded...

"Oh hi – I'm sorry – I needed to use the bathroom..."

"I SAID GET OUT!" This bitch looked at my husband and waited for him to say something – the fuck?!

"I'll see you downstairs..." he told her. I went the fuck off...

WHY THE FUCK WAS SHE IN OUR BEDROOM?!"

"You heard her – she needed to use the bathroom..." he answered non-chalantly...

"SHE HAS NO FUCKING BUSINESS IN OUR BEDROOM! PERIOD! WHAT THE FUCK IS WRONG WITH YOU?!"

"WHO THE FUCK DO YOU THINK YOU'RE TALKING TO?!" he gritted as he grabbed my throat and began squeezing...

"YYY... OOO... UUU... MMM... UUU... TTT... HHH... AAA... FFF... UUU... CCC... KKK... AAA..." I managed to squeeze out. I was too angry to be scared and it surprised him...

"You're lucky I love you..." he breathed before he kissed me...

"Let go of me..."

"I'll see you downstairs..." he said as he let go of my throat. I stood in front of the bed and watched him leave as if nothing happened. I waited for him to close the door and I hurried to lock it. After I locked the door I went to look in the mirror...

"SHIT!" I exclaimed when I saw his handprint around my throat...

"Is everything alright?" she asked as he walked into the living room...

"Everything's fine..."

"Where's Mommy?" Billy asked...

"I'm right here..." Dawn answered...

"Not you Mommy – Demi..."

"I told you not to call her that!" she snapped...

"But you said we were family..." he said as he started to cry...

"I'm right here Baby..." I answered as I went to hug him but Dawn pulled him into a hug before I could...

"I'm sorry..." she lied... "You're right – we're family – you can call her Mommy if you want to..." she said as she looked at me with daggers in her eyes...

"Okay..." he sniffed...

"What are you cooking?" William asked as if he didn't see what just happened...

"I'm making lasagna..."

"I'm not in the mood for lasagna – cook something else..."

"I'm sorry Honey – everything else is frozen – if I had known earlier I would've taken something else out..." I said as I went into the kitchen...

"I'll help you thaw something else out..." Dawn said as she got up...

"No you won't – we're having lasagna – besides – it's getting late – don't you need to be getting home?" I suggested on purpose...

"Can Mommy stay for dinner?"

"Not tonight – I want to have dinner with you and Daddy – Mommy can stay another night..."

"Okay..." he sighed...

"Billy – go in the office and start on your homework..." my husband commanded...

"Okay Daddy..." I already knew what was coming...

"Demi – come in here and sit down – we need to talk..."

"I need to keep an eye on the food..." I lied. I knew it wouldn't work, but it was all I could think of...

"I said come here..." I didn't even realize he got up to come in the kitchen...

"Fine..." I relented. I turned the flame down to simmer so I could get this over with without burning the food. When we got in the living room, I sat down on the other side of him...

"We need to get on the same page..." he started to say...

"Damn right we do..." I added...

"Shut up – I'm not done talking..."

"Go ahead..." Dawn said...

"You need to understand something Demi – we're family – whether you like it or not – you knew what it was when you married me – Dawn is his mother – she's welcome here anytime – that's how co-parenting works – have I made myself clear?" Dawn was sitting there beaming from ear to ear but she had no idea what was coming...

"Are you done?" I asked...

"We'll be done when you acknowledge that you understand what the fuck I just said..."

"Mmm hmm... – okay – first of all – the definition of co-parenting is two parents doing what's best for the child – in the child's interest – co-parenting is not Dawn being welcome to drop by whenever she feels like it as if she's still married to you..."

"Wait a minute..." Dawn interrupted...

"Shut up – I'm not done – anyway – as I was saying – Dawn is Billy's mother – she is welcome to see her son, help her son with his homework, attend events, join PTA, attend teacher conferences..."

"I don't need your permission..."

"Will you please shut up?!" I exclaimed as I continued... "Co-parenting does not mean I have to welcome Dawn showing up unannounced, helping herself to whatever is in the refrigerator as if she put food in there, staying for dinner as if we're sister wives, or being in our bedroom – she is not your wife – I am – and you both need to understand that..." I said as I turned to her and continued... "And you need to respect those boundaries – matter of fact – Billy – your mother is leaving – come tell her good night!" Billy came running out to say good night to his mother before either of them could react...

"Good night Mommy..." he said as he hugged her...

"Good night – I'll see you tomorrow..." she said as she got up to leave...

"Good night..." I said as she opened the door and left. I got up, closed the door, and locked it...

"Smells good – what's for dinner Mommy?"

"I'm making lasagna..." I answered as I went back into the kitchen. I knew my husband was pissed and I didn't give a fuck. I also knew I might pay for it later – and I didn't give a fuck about that either...

"I don't know who the fuck that bitch thinks she is talking to me like that – she's lucky my son was there or I would 'a bust that ass!" she exclaimed out loud to no one as she parked her car. Her phone alerted her to a text from my husband as soon as she put her key in the door... "He can wait until I get in the house..." she said as she unlocked the door and went inside. She took her coat off, tossed it on the couch, went into the kitchen, poured herself a glass of wine, and took a sip before she took her phone out and started reading...

"I'm sorry. I don't know what her problem is. We'll talk tomorrow morning after she leaves. Come by at 8..."

"I don't think so..." she said out loud as she lifted her glass, took another cup of wine, put the glass down, and replied to his message...

"You know exactly what her problem is! You didn't even bother to check her – you just let her talk to me however she wanted!"

"I'm sorry. I'll make it up to you when you get here tomorrow..."

"So you think you can just fuck your way out of this one huh?"

"Don't I always?"

"That shit may work on her, but it won't work on me – I'm not your wife – remember?"

"Stop it – you know you still want this dick – come get it..."

"Fuck you William!"

"I'll see you tomorrow..."

"Dinner's ready..." I said as I took the lasagna out the oven...

"I already told you I don't want that shit..." he mumbled...

"Good – 'cause I'm hungry!" Billy exclaimed...

"Come sit at the table – I'll make us a plate..." I said as I took two plates down from the cabinet...

"What about Daddy? You forgot his plate..."

"Daddy doesn't want any lasagna..." I sighed. Billy went to sit at the table and waited as I made the plates. I brought them to the table and sat down with him as William opened the refrigerator...

"Watcha doin' Daddy?"

"Makin' a sandwich..." I shook my head at Billy and he understood to leave his father alone...

"I'll be upstairs..." he said as he left the kitchen. I waited for him to go upstairs before I spoke...

"Billy – how'd you like to have your bedroom downstairs instead of upstairs?"

"Am I in trouble?"

"No Billy..."

"Then why do you want my room to be moved downstairs?"

"Well..." I paused as I hurried to come up with something... "I was thinking it would be easier for you..."

"It's not hard for me to go upstairs..."

"I know – but when you come home from school – sometimes you have to go to the bathroom – you throw your stuff on the couch – you go to the bathroom – then you have to come out the bathroom – Daddy tells you go back and wash your hands – you go back and wash your hands – Daddy says get your stuff off the couch – you take your things upstairs – then you have to bring your things downstairs to do your homework – then back upstairs again – I was thinking it would be easier if you had your room downstairs so you wouldn't have to go up and down the stairs so much..." We continued to eat as he sat there thinking about what I said. I smiled to myself as I knew I had him...

"What about your office?"

"I'll move my office upstairs to your room..."

"What if I need to use the computer? Won't I have to go upstairs anyway?" Damn this kid was smart...

"I'll buy you a computer and your desk will be in your room so you won't have to do that..."

"You will?!"

"Yes..."

"Yeeaaa! Thank you! I can't wait to tell Daddy!"

"Don't tell Daddy..."

"Don't tell Daddy? Why?"

"I want it to be a surprise..."

"Oohhh..." We continued to eat and then he spoke again... "Mommy?"

"Yes Baby..."

"Won't Daddy know if he helps you move my room downstairs?"

"No – I'm going to do it tomorrow when Daddy goes to work..."

"But don't you have to work tomorrow?"

"I'm taking the day off..."

"Oohhh... Okay..."

"Remember – you can't tell Daddy – okay?"

"Okay..."

"Don't tell me what?" William asked as he came into the kitchen...

"Mommy has a surprise – ooppss..."

"Oh yea?" he asked as he looked at me mischievously...

"Yea..." I sighed...

"So when do I get my surprise?"

"Tonight – Billy – put your plate in the sink – you need to get ready for school tomorrow..."

"But I didn't have anything to drink!"

"Take a juice out the refrigerator – you can drink it upstairs while you get ready for bed..."

"Okay!" he squealed as he jumped up, put his plate in the sink, snatched the refrigerator open, grabbed a juice, slammed the door shut, and hurried upstairs...

"Stop slammin' doors in this house!" William boomed...

"Sorry Daddy!" he yelled from the top of the stairs.

"*N*ow... about my surprise..." he said as he came over to me and pulled me into his arms...

"Yeess..." I sighed...

"I want it here..." he breathed as he kissed my neck... "And I want it now..." he breathed as he unbuckled his pants...

"William... we can't... Billy could come downstairs..." I pleaded...

"You know we can hear him if he comes downstairs..." he whispered as he palmed my ass...

"What if he sneaks downstairs? Please... I don't want us to get caught..."

"You get on my fuckin' nerves..." he mumbled as he fixed himself and let go of me...

"Wait a minute – why don't we go in the office – we can lock the door so if he comes downstairs he won't catch us..."

"That'll work..." he growled as he grabbed my hand and pulled me behind him...

"Lock the door..." I did as I was told... "Come over here..." I went to stand in front of him... "Bend your ass over that desk..." I moved in front of the desk, bent myself over, and braced myself. I heard the zipper and I spread my legs before he could tell me to... "That's my girl..." he said as he pulled my pants down off my waist along with my panties... "Are you ready to give me my surprise?" he breathed as he bent over on my back...

"Yeess..." I moaned as he entered me...

"Oh yea... You're ready..." he breathed in my ear as he began pounding. The desk was scraping the floor so hard if it wasn't for the carpet underneath, it would've hit the wall and my fingers would've been bleeding... "Ugh! Ugh! Ugh!" I was coming all over his dick as he started talking shit... "Is this my pussy?"

"Yes Daddy! Yes!"

"Damn right it is – you love this dick – don't you!"

"Yes Daddy! Yes!"

"Tell me to fuck you!"

"Fuck me Daddy! Just like that!"

"Tell me you don't want me to stop!"

"Don't stop Daddy! Don't stop!"

"Cum for me!"

"I'm cumming Daddy! I'm cumming!"

"Uggh! Uggh! Uggh! Uggh! Uuuggghhh!" He collapsed on top of me with his dick still inside and he continued to lay on top of me as his cum dripped down my legs...

"That was nice..." he breathed...

"You're welcome..."

"I want more when we get upstairs..." he said as he got up off me...

"Okay..." I sighed as I stood up, turned around, and pulled up my pants...

"Go wash your ass..." he said before he unlocked the door and left the office. I waited until he went upstairs before I went into the bathroom...

"I could'a washed my ass upstairs mutha fucka..." I mumbled as I turned the water on... "Fuck this — I'm taking a shower..." I said as I turned on the water. I waited until it was good and hot before I got in. I closed the shower door, closed my eyes, and began to fantasize about Dante as the water hit my body... "I'm cumming Dante..." I whispered as I played with my clit. It never took long for me to cum when I fantasized about him. I pushed my fingers inside and began to moan as I hit my g-spot... "Dante... Dante... Dante..."

"What the hell are you doing?!" I was so caught up in my fantasy I didn't even hear William come in the bathroom...

"I... I decided to take a shower..." I stammered...

"You could'a took a shower upstairs!"

"I was going to – but you told me to wash my ass – remember?" I answered as I put body wash on the loofah and began washing myself as water splashed on him and the floor...

"Hurry up – I want some more pussy before I go to bed..." he said as he closed the shower door...

"William – wait..."

"What?" he asked as he opened the shower door...

"Why don't you join me?"

"I'll be upstairs..." he answered as he closed the shower door again. I didn't bother to stop him this time – I hurried up and rinsed myself off. I wrapped a towel around myself, took the robe off the door, put it on, and hurried upstairs...

"Bout time you got up here..." he said as he propped his head up on his hand and elbow. I dropped the robe, dropped the towel, and went towards the bed... "Get your ass in here..." he commanded. I did as he commanded and got under the covers. He didn't waste any time getting on top of me – but this time, he engaged in a bit of foreplay... "You know I don't like to be kept waiting..." he whispered as he spread my legs...

"I know..." I breathed as he began licking and sucking my breasts. He took my left nipple in his mouth and began to suck on it hard... "Oohhh..."

"You like that?"

"Yeess..." I moaned as he took my right nipple in his mouth and sucked it just as hard... "Ooohhh..." He continued sucking as he moved his hand down my body...

"Mmm..." he moaned as he spread my legs with his hand...

"Yeess..." I moaned as he began playing with my clit...

"You like that?"

"Yeess..." I moaned as he pushed his fingers inside...

"Fuck my hand..." he commanded as he began massaging my g-spot...

"Ohh... Oh... Oh..." I moaned...

"Yea... That's it... Cum on my hand..."

"Ohh... Oh... Oh... Oh... Ooohhh..." he continued massaging my g-spot and I was sensitive... "William... I can't..."

"You can..." he breathed as he massaged harder...

"Oh William... Oh... Shit..."

"There it is..." he breathed as I squirted all over his hand. I was in a daze as he got on top of me and thrust himself inside me...

"Huh... Huh... Huh..."

"Uggh! Uggh! Ugh!"

"Huh... Huh... Huh..."

"Uggh! Uggh! Ugh! Uggh! Uuuggghhh!" He collapsed on top of me and I lay perfectly still until he began to snore...

"Sleep well..." I whispered as I pushed him off me as gently as I could. As soon as his head hit the pillow, he hugged the pillow, slid off me, and fell deeper into his nightly coma...

"Don't stop Dante!" she cried...

"I'ma stop!"

"Don't you dare fuckin' stop! I'm cumming!"

"I'ma stop!"

"Fuck me mutha fucka! I'm cumming! Aaahhh!"

"Uggh! Uggh! Ugh! Uggh! Uuuggghhh!"

"Oh Dante..." Dawn whispered with tears in her eyes...

"I love you..." he said as he kissed her...

"I love you too..." she breathed...

"You love this dick..." he breathed as he continued kissing her...

"Yes Baby... I love your dick..."

"You want some more... don't you?"

"Yes Baby... Yes..."

"I'm sorry Baby... I'd love to... But I need to get some sleep – I have an early meeting..." he breathed as he stopped, rolled off of her, and turned his back to her...

"Dante..." she whispered. He started snoring, pretending to be asleep so she would leave him alone...

"Works every time..." she sighed as she slid down and spooned him. Dante smiled to himself as he closed his eyes and dreamed of me.

I made sure I set my alarm before we went to bed so I could get in the shower before I got dressed... "Good morning..." William said as he smiled...

"Good morning..." I greeted as I continued getting dressed. He got up out the bed, came over to me, and blocked me from moving. His dick was standing at attention... "Since you're up early... why don't we get a quickie in?" he breathed as he kissed me...

"I wish we could... but I can't..."

"Whyyy..." he moaned in my mouth...

"Because... we don't do quickies..."

"You're right..."

"Billy will wind up being late for school..."

"True..."

"We can go to bed early tonight..."

"That sounds good…" he breathed as he kissed me again. He pulled me closer and held me as his dick pressed against me…

"Stop it…" I laughed…

"No…"

"Mommy?" Billy called out from his room…

"I'm coming!" I exclaimed as I pulled away from William and hurried out the room… "You're dressed already…"

"Are we still doing the surprise?" he whispered…

"Yes… Sshh…"

"Okay Mommy…"

"Good morning Billy…"

"Good morning Daddy…"

"You're already dressed…"

"Yes – I'm…"

"He's really excited to go to school – c'mon Billy…" I interrupted as I took his hand and pulled him towards the stairs…

"I'm coming Mommy…" he laughed. William followed us downstairs and I went into the kitchen to make coffee…

"What's going on Billy?" he asked as he moved towards him…

"It's a surprise…"

"C'mon… you can tell me…"

"You'll find out later today when you get home…" I interrupted as I handed him a cup of coffee…

"Thank you…"

"You're welcome – Billy – get your coat – I'm taking you to school early..."

"Okay..."

"Is that because you're surprising me?" William asked...

"Yes – I'll see you later..." I stopped to give him a quick kiss, took Billy by the hand, and hurried out the house...

"That was close Mommy..." Billy laughed...

"I know – that's why I'm taking you to school early..."

"Oohhh..."

"Hey..." he answered...

"I'm on my way..."

"Don't come..."

"Why?"

"She's up to something..."

"Is she on to us?"

"I don't think so..."

"What makes you think she's up to something?"

"She planning a surprise – she's been planning it since last night – and Billy's in on it..."

"Oh no – I think I know what it is..."

"What do you think it is?"

"She's pregnant..."

"You think so?"

"Yes – especially because Billy's in on it..." William began to smile... "Hello? Are you still there?"

"I'm here..."

"I'm going to go into work – I'll see you tonight..."

"See you tonight..." he said and then he hung up abruptly...

"I hope that bitch isn't pregnant..." she sighed as she made a U-turn and headed into work...

"William? Honey are you here?" I held my breath waiting for him to answer and I let out a sigh of relief when he didn't answer...

"Where do we start?" Reggie asked. Reggie was recommended to me by Dante and I was grateful...

"The office is in here..." I answered as I went towards the office and he followed...

"This isn't too bad – if you have a few boxes for the loose papers I can move this quick..."

"Come upstairs – I'll show you Billy's room..." Reggie followed me upstairs and into Billy's room... "Oh this is easy – he keeps his room clean – I'll take the drawers out the dresser, move the dresser downstairs, and then I'll come back upstairs and get the drawers – can you get the closet and the toy box?"

"I can take care of the closet but I can't do the toy box..."

"Don't worry – I gotchu..." he said as he went over to the dresser and began to take out the drawers, and put them on the bed...

"Thank you so much – I really appreciate this..."

"You're welcome – I'm glad he doesn't have bunk beds – they're a pain in the ass to move..."

"Have you had breakfast?"

"No I haven't – but if you're offering – I accept..."

"You got it – I'll place an order with Bagel King..."

"I'll take a steak, egg, and cheese on a bagel and a black coffee..."

"Got it..." I said as he went back to what he was doing...

"Excuse me..." he said as he picked up the dresser...

"Sorry..."

"You don't need to apologize..." he said as he moved past me and carried the dresser downstairs. I followed behind him...

"Where are you putting the dresser?"

"I'm going to put the furniture in here first. I'll move the office upstairs and then we'll move the furniture from the living room into his new bedroom..."

"Oh – okay..." I sat down and watched him go upstairs and then I checked my phone...

"I thought you were going to help..." he laughed as he came back downstairs...

"Breakfast is here..." I said as I got up, went to the door, picked up the bag, and brought it in the house... "C'mon – take a break and come with me..." Reggie followed me into the kitchen and we sat down at the table...

"Thank you..."

"You're welcome." We didn't say anything else as we ate... "Oh shoot – that's my phone..." I exclaimed as I hurried to answer it...

"Hey Demi..."

"Hey..."

"Why are you out of breath?"

"Umm – I'm in the middle of something – I'll call you back later – bye..."

"Was that your husband?"

"Yea..."

"He's not going to show up here – is he?"

"He might..."

"Do I need to be worried?"

"Naa – I told him I had a surprise for him..."

"Okay – let's get back to work..." he said as he went back upstairs. I followed him and began removing Billy's clothes from the closet... "Before we start on the office – do you want that desk down here and the desk in there upstairs?"

"Yes..."

"I thought you'd say that..."

"Is that going to be a problem?"

"No – it's just going to take a bit longer – I need to take the desk apart down here and put it back together upstairs..."

"I'm sorry..."

"You don't need to apologize – we'll get this done – we'll take the things off the desk and take out the drawers – I'll take the desk apart, take the pieces upstairs, put it back together, and then I'll put the drawers back in it..."

"Thank God you're here..." I sighed. Reggie smiled at me and then I followed him into the office. I grabbed a box and started taking papers off the desk...

"I'm going to take these boxes out the closet and put them in front of the door so we can go back and forth..."

"Uh huh – okay..." I couldn't believe what I found.

"My Worst Nightmare..." I read out loud...

"Did you say something?"

"On no – I just found something I thought I lost..." I lied. I put the manuscript inside the box and covered it with the rest of the papers on the desk so nobody would find it, and then I took the box upstairs. When I came back downstairs, Reggie already had the closet cleared out...

"You ready for the next step?"

"Yes..."

"Okay – I'll take the drawers out the credenza – you take the drawers out the desk..."

"Okay..." I couldn't stop thinking about the title. 'My Worst Nightmare' kept flashing in my mind as we continued to work. When we got all the furniture in my new office, I looked around and sighed... "I should've done this a long time ago..."

"I think this is a better room for you..."

"Me too..."

"Okay — I'll put this desk together while you put the clothes and other things in your son's new room..."

"Okay..." I went downstairs and I was in a great mood... "You're going to be happy in this room Billy..." I said out loud as I finished putting everything in the closet...

"Do you want the computer and printer to go upstairs?"

"Yes I do..."

"Okay — I'll get those set up for you..." I waited for Reggie to take the computer upstairs and then I decided to put the bed in the room... "Uh uh — I'll get that..."

"Okay..." I watched Reggie as he brought the desk into the room first, followed by the drawers... "I thought you were going to bring the bed in first..."

"The bed takes up the most room so it always goes in last..."

"Okay..." I followed him into Billy's new room and watched him position the desk... "I'm going to leave the desk here in front of the window so you can set up his game, a computer, and a printer..."

"He'll like that..."

"Okay — why don't you go upstairs — I'll meet you up there in a few..."

"Okay..." I went upstairs, went into my new office, and took out her manuscript... "I can't believe you were working on a book like you still live here..." I said out loud as I started reading...

"I thought I'd met the love of my life. Everything was fine as long as it went his way. I should warn her but fuck her – it's not like we're friends. She's lucky I'm cordial to her – but I guess I have to do that for my son. Every time I hear him call her Mommy it makes me cringe – and she eats it right up..."

"Hey..."

"Oh – sorry – I was just..."

"Where would you like me to put the credenza?"

"I want the credenza over here where the connection is – I'll put my desk in front of the window..."

"Okay – I'll be right back..." he said as he went back downstairs. I picked up right where I left off...

"Thank God he hasn't cut me out of my son's life – he's the one good thing that came out of our marriage..."

"Excuse me..."

"Oh – sorry..." I moved out the way and he put the credenza down...

"I'm going to bring the drawers upstairs – they're not as heavy as the credenza..."

"Do you want me to empty the drawers?"

"You don't mind?"

"No – I'll take the stuff out..." I said as I followed him downstairs. He waited for me to finish taking the stuff out the bottom drawer and then he took it upstairs. When he came back downstairs he started helping me pick up what I took out the bottom drawer... "Thank you..."

"You're welcome..." We headed upstairs, I put the stuff in the drawer, and then we went back downstairs...

"Ready for the top drawer?"

"Yea..." I answered as I started taking everything out the drawer. Reggie waited for me to finish and then he took the drawer upstairs. I waited for him to come back down and then we both took the stuff upstairs...

"Do you have a hand truck?"

"Yes..."

"Mind if I use it?"

"Not at all – it's in the garage..." I answered as I opened the garage for him...

"Did you just open the garage?"

"Yea..." I answered as we went outside. Reggie took the hand truck inside and put a piece of the desk on it...

"I'll bump this piece upstairs first – it's the heaviest..."

"Okay..." I watched him swivel and move the hand truck around and I was impressed. I heard a thump when he put the desk down... "Is everything alright?"

"Everything's fine..."

"Okay..." He bumped the hand truck downstairs and put the last piece of the desk on it...

"This is the last piece – when I come back downstairs, I'll put the boxes on the hand truck so we can get them upstairs faster..."

"Okay..." I heard another thump and then it was quiet... "Are you okay?"

"I'm okay – I'm putting your desk together..."

"Okay..." I picked up the computer and took it upstairs...

"What made you get an all-in-one computer?"

"I like to stretch my legs under the desk..."

"Hmmm – I never thought of that..."

"It makes things easier for me – I just go from left to right – and when I want to play music or rip a cd – it's on the right..."

"I might get myself one..."

"Could you do me a favor?"

"Sure..."

"Could you set up the computer, Wi-Fi, and printer for me?"

"I can do that – I'll do that after I bring up the boxes..." he answered as he rolled himself out from under the desk...

"Thanks..."

"Okay – let's go get those boxes..." he said before he headed downstairs with the hand truck. I watched him put the boxes on the hand truck and then he started up the stairs... "What are you doing?"

"I'm making sure the boxes don't fall because you don't have a belt..."

"Okay..." When we got upstairs, he put all the boxes on the floor...

"Do I need to put these in the closet in any particular order?"

"No..."

"Okay..." I watched him put the boxes in the closet and I noticed I had more room...

"I didn't realize how big this closet was..."

"This really is the better room for your office..."

"I can't believe we're just about finished..."

"I'll set up your computer, Wi-Fi, and printer now..."

"Okay..."

"Do you want me to bring this chair downstairs and bring the other chair upstairs?"

"Yes..."

"Okay – I'll do that as soon as I'm done with this..." I continued to watch him intently. I wasn't sure whether I wanted to shred the book or read it – and then I remembered the shredder was downstairs...

"I'll be right back..." I said and then I hurried downstairs. I went into the room, picked up the shredder, and brought it upstairs...

"You're all set..."

"Thank you..." Reggie picked up the chair and I followed him back downstairs. We went into Billy's new room and I looked around... "I sure hope he likes his new room..."

"He'll like it – could you roll this chair into the living room? I'm going to put the bed in here now..."

"Okay..." Reggie didn't wait for me to get out of his way – he went past me and picked up the frame...

"You need help with that?'

"Naa – I got it..." I went to sit down and waited for him to finish putting the bed in the room... "Come take a look..." I got up and went inside..."

"Aww... you made the bed..."

"You like it?"

"I love it – I just hope he likes it..."

"He will – do you need me to come back and hook up his game or his computer?'

"No – my husband will do that..."

"Okay – I have another job to get to – if you ever need me for anything else – have Dante reach out to me..."

"I will – thanks again – oh wait – how much do I owe you?'

"Dante already took care of it..." he answered as he opened the door and left.

"*H*ey..." he answered...

"Hey Dante..."

"How'd everything go?"

"It went great..."

"Good..."

"I'm going to pay you back..."

"No you're not..."

"I need to tell you something..."

"You need to tell me you love me?" he laughed...

"Dante – I'm serious..."

"Oh no – what's wrong?"

"Dawn has been using my office for her personal business..."

"She doesn't have a business..."

"She's writing a book..."

"She is?!"

"I found her manuscript..."

"Did you read it?"

"I started to..."

"What's it about?"

"It's about us..."

"Us?"

"The title is My Worst Nightmare. I started reading it and she talks about how she cringes every time she hears Billy call me Mommy..."

"WHAT?!"

"She also said I'm lucky she's cordial to me..."

"What a bitch!"

"I knew she didn't like me and I don't like her either – but now that I read some of her book – it all makes sense..."

"It does?"

"Yea – she's bitter because she lost William..."

"She's the one that wanted the divorce!"

"Maybe so – but she said thought she'd met the love of her life..."

"Uh huh..."

"She said something else that worries me..."

"What did she say?"

"She said she should warn me – but fuck me..."

"WHAT?!"

"Yea..."

"Wait... Wait... Wait... – she smiles in your face – she pretends to help Billy with his homework – and the whole time she's been using your office to write a book?!"

"That's not the only thing she's doing..."

"What else is there?!"

"I came home from work the other day and she was upstairs in the bedroom with William..."

"You caught them fucking?!"

"No – they were talking and laughing – I went into the bedroom and she said she needed to pee..."

"What the fuck?!"

"Exactly!"

"You should've told her to get the fuck out!"

"I did – and I went off on William and cursed him out... and..."

"What happened?"

"He choked me..."

"HE WHAT?!"

"Yea..."

"Oh my God... Demi... I'm so sorry..."

"I'm not..."

"Wait – what?"

"I'm not sorry – I said what I said and I didn't give a fuck – I was too angry to be scared – to be honest – I think it turned him on..."

"Did he hurt you?"

"He left his hand print on my throat – but I'm okay now..." Dante wasn't speaking but I knew he was angry – I could tell by his breathing...

"Is that why you moved Billy's room downstairs?"

"Yea..."

"I'm sorry you're going through this – you deserve so much better..."

"Don't say anything..."

"Fuck that – I'm saying something to her as soon as she gets home!"

"Dante no – please don't..."

"Okay – I won't say anything – for you..."

"What would I do without you?"

"You'll never have to find out..."

"I'm going to shred her manuscript..."

"Are you going to finish reading it first?"

"No – I've read enough..."

"Are you going to tell William?"

"No..."

"What if she tells you she left something in the office?"

"She won't say anything to me because that'll expose her..."

"You're right – but what if she accesses the computer when she's helping Billy with his homework?"

"I'm going to move my documents to an external drive. I'm also going to buy Billy his own computer and printer – and I'll have access to his computer so I can delete anything she creates that has nothing to do with his homework..."

"Make sure you scrub your computer too – she might have access to your files from her laptop..."

"Okay..."

"I need to get back to work – we'll talk later..."

"Okay – later..." I sat there for a few moments thinking about our conversation and then I went into Billy's new room...

"Let's see what you have in here..." I said as I went through the desk drawers... "Nothing but school supplies in here..." I said and then I started going through his dresser. I went through everything and was relieved that all I found was clothes. I went upstairs and started going through the desk... "Hmm – this notebook has got to go..." I said. I went through the other drawers and I found an old letter written to William. I took it out the envelope and started reading...

"I'll be home late. I have a project I need to finish. I'll make it up to you when I get home. I love you. Love Dawn..."

I saw that it was dated six months before we were married... "This can go too..." I said as I turned on the computer... "Hmmm – thanks for not erasing the internet history..." I said as I scrolled through the searches. After I erased the history I cleared all the cookies and then I checked my C Drive... "Well, well, well – look at these..." I said as I deleted all the saved copies of her book. I scrolled down the list of documents in the drive to make sure there was nothing else, I emptied my waste basket so nothing could be retrieved, and then I connected my external hard drive, moved all my documents onto it, and disconnected it. I decided to check my email and when I went to Yahoo, I saw that she was in her email recently and didn't log out. Curiosity got the best of me and I went in her inbox. I regretted it as soon as I saw the first email...

"*HE CHEATED ON ME*!!!"

I scrolled down and saw a lot of emails between her and William. I should've deleted them but curiosity got the best of me again and, again, I regretted it as soon as I opened it...

"I thought you loved her..."
"I do..."
"Why are you cheating on her then?"

I clicked off the email and burst into tears... "NO – I'M NOT GOING TO DO THIS!" I exclaimed as I wiped my tears. I decided I was going to fuck her up good. First, I did a mass delete of everything in her inbox. Once I was done with that, I went to her sent messages and, again, I was disappointed... "I'm not reading anymore..." I said as I shook my head back and forth. I deleted all the sent emails too.... "And now I'm changing the password..." I said. I laughed as I came up with the perfect password: FuckYouBitch24! "I hope this takes..." I said as I filled out the request for a new password... "Yes!" I exclaimed as it was accepted. I got up from the desk, shredded her manuscript and the old letter I found, and then I put a password on my computer... "Good luck getting in here now bitch..." I said as I got up and went downstairs...

"Hey..."

"Hey..." I whispered as I started crying...

"Demi... What's wrong?"

"He's cheating on me..."

"Are you sure?"

"She's been using my computer to send emails – she sent an email to William asking him why he was cheating on me if he loves me..."

"I'm so sorry..."

"I love him so much..."

"I know..."

"I found an old letter she wrote him..."

"What did you do with it?"

"I shredded it with her manuscript..."

"Is she still logged into her email?"

"No – I emptied her inbox, I emptied her sent items, I emptied her trash, and then I changed her password..."

"What about your computer?"

"I cleared the internet history, I deleted the cookies, I deleted her documents from my C Drive, I moved all my documents to my external hard drive, and I put a password on my computer..."

"Good..."

"I need to go – I have to get Billy from school..."

"What are you going to do when she wants to help Billy with his homework?"

"I'm going to act as if I have no idea what the fuck she's talking about..."

"What are you going to do about William?"

"Nothing..."

"Nothing?! He's cheating on you!"

"I love him! I'm not just going to throw what we have away!"

"You go get Billy – we'll talk later..." he said as he hung up... "How the hell can I tell her he's cheating on her with his ex-wife?" he sighed.

"$\mathcal{H}$ i Mommy!"

"Hi Billy – how was your day?"

"Did you do the surprise?"

"Yes..."

"Did Daddy see it?"

"Not yet..."

"I hope Daddy likes it..."

"I'm sure he will – but we need to make a stop before we get home..." I said as I put on my seat belt...

"Where are we going Mommy?"

"You'll see..." Billy sat there quiet and looked out the window as I called William...

"Hello Demi..."

"Hi Daddy!" Billy exclaimed...

"Are you on your way home?"

"Not yet – I need to make a stop first..."

"How long will you be?'

"I won't be long Honey…"

"Okay – I'll see you soon…"

"See you soon – I love you…"

"I love you too…"

"I love you Daddy!"

"I love you too Billy…"   Billy was beaming from ear to ear as we went down the highway. It was a shame he didn't hear that from his father more often…

"Best… Buy…" he read…

"That's right…" I continued as I parked the car…

"Are we going to Best Buy?"

"Yes Billy…"

"Welcome to Best Buy – how can I help you today?"

"I'm looking for a Hewlett Packard All-in-One…"

"Come with me…" the associate said as he motioned for us to follow him…

"Mommy – can I get a game?"

"Not today Billy…"

"How's this?" the associate asked…

"I like it…"

"It's an HP24 All-in-One – it has…"

"That's okay – I have one at home…"

"You do?"

"Yes…"

"This one has the Windows 11 operating system, webcam, blue tooth, Wi-Fi…"

"Is that the price?"

"Yes – it's $359.99…"

"Do you have a printer to go with it?"

"How's this one?"

"Hmm – a Desk Jet All-in-One with bonus 6 months of instant ink for $69.99?"

"Yes..."

"I'll take the computer and the printer..."

"Great! I'll take care of these for you – I'll meet you at the front..."

"Thank you..."

"You're welcome!"

"Billy?"

"Yes Mommy?"

"I know I said I would buy you a new computer – but Mommy needs this one – is it okay if I take this one and give you the one I have at home?"

"Yes Mommy..."

"Thank you Billy..."

"Can I keep the new printer?"

"Yes..."

"Okay..." We walked up to the counter and the associate was all smiles as I took out my credit card and handed it to him...

"You're all set – have a great evening..."

"Thank you – you too..."

"Hmmm – what's this?" William asked as he looked at the alert from American Express...

"*Did you make this purchase? Check Yes or No to confirm...*"

"Hmmm – I guess Demi needed a new computer and printer..." he said as he clicked yes to confirm the purchase...

"*Thanks for confirming!*"

"Hi Mommy! Hi Daddy!" Billy exclaimed as we came inside...

"Hi Billy – where were you?' Dawn asked...

"I went with Mommy to buy a new computer!"

"Oh – is there something wrong with the old one?" she asked nervously...

"No – I promised Billy I would get him his own computer but I decided to keep it for myself since it comes with Windows 11..." I answered...

"So you're going to give Billy the computer you're using now?" William asked...

"Yes – but Billy's also getting a new printer..."

"Oh wow – that's nice – what brought this on?"

"Can I tell Daddy about the surprise Mommy?"

"Yes Billy..."

"Mommy moved my room down here so I don't have to go upstairs anymore!"

"What?!" Dawn exclaimed. William looked at me side-eyed...

"Mommy said it would be easier for me so when I come home from school I could just put my things in my room and you can help me with my homework in my room because I have a computer! Can I go see my new room Mommy?"

"Of course..." I answered...

"Okay!" he exclaimed as he ran into his room... "Mommy! I like it!"

"You do?"

"Yes! Come see Mommy!" Dawn got up from the couch and went into Billy's new room. William just continued to look at me...

"Honey – could you help me set up the new computer upstairs?"

"I'll do that later..."

"Okay – I'll bring this upstairs – I'm going to bring the old computer downstairs so Dawn can help Billy with his homework – could you help me set up the computer and printer for Billy?"

"I guess I can do that..."

"Okay – I'll be right back..."

"Billy?"

"Yes Mommy?"

"When did Demi tell you she was moving your room downstairs?"

"Yesterday..."

"Did Daddy know?"

"No Mommy – it was a surprise..."

"A surprise? For who?"

"A surprise for Daddy..."

"Surprise for Daddy my ass..." she mumbled...

"What did you say Mommy?"

"Nothing – I'm glad you like your room..."

"This will be quick..." I said as I removed my external hard drive and disconnected my old computer...

"Demi..."

"William! You scared me!"

"I know what you're up to..."

"What are you talking about?" I asked nervously...

"You moved Billy's room downstairs because of what happened yesterday..." he said as he sat on the desk...

"Yes..." I sighed...

"And you told Billy it was a surprise so he wouldn't tell me..."

"Yea..."

"You had my son lie to me..."

"That's not true – it was a surprise – it was a surprise for you because you didn't know..."

"You lied to me..."

"I didn't lie to you – I just didn't tell you what I was doing..."

"When I called you earlier today – you told me you were in the middle of something..."

"I was..."

"Were you alone?"

"No..."

"So you had another man in my house..."

"Yes..."

"So that's how you got this done..."

"Yes..."

"You should've told me..."

"I couldn't tell you..."

"Why?"

"The last time I told you how I felt about Dawn being in our bedroom... you choked me..."

"Excuse me?" Dawn interrupted as she came into the office...

"Dawn – we'll talk to you downstairs..." William said...

"I need to help Billy with his homework and..."

"What the fuck did he just tell you?!" I exclaimed...

"Fine!" she exclaimed as she stomped back downstairs...

"This is why I didn't tell you!" I exclaimed as I snatched the computer off my desk and took it downstairs. William followed behind me...

"*H*ey..."

"Hi Mommy – are you going to hook up my computer now?" Billy asked as I came in...

"I'm going to do it..." William answered as he took the computer from me, put it on the desk, and connected it to the outlet... "Nice printer..." he sighed as he took it out the box. Dawn was seething and I didn't give a fuck... "Okay – you're all set – let's turn this on..." I watched and waited...

"It's locked..." Dawn said...

"Yes – I know – I put a password on it..."

"Why would you do that?!" she snapped...

"It keeps Billy from accessing the computer when he's not supposed to..." I answered. She had no idea I knew why she was asking...

"Well could you put the password in so I can help him with his homework?! I don't have all night!"

"Sure..." I answered slyly. It was hard for me to keep a straight face as I went over to the computer... "Do you mind?!" I snapped as she looked over my shoulder...

"I need to know the password so I can help him when you're not here!"

"I'll always be here..." I said deliberately as I covered the keys so she couldn't see what I typed in...

"Finally!" she exclaimed...

"Honey?"

"Yes Demi?"

"Could you come upstairs with me and help me set up my new computer while she helps Billy with his homework?"

"Sure..." he answered. I left Billy's room and he followed...

"What's wrong Mommy?" Billy asked...

"I can't find it! Shit!"

"Are you looking for my homework?"

"No – I'm looking for something else..." she answered as she searched frantically on the C Drive...

"Mommy?"

"Yes Billy?"

"Can you help me with this?" he asked as he handed her a paper...

"This is math..."

"I know – but it's hard..."

"Do what you can – I'll go over it after you're finished..."

"Okay..." Dawn went to yahoo and tried to log into her email...

"What is with technology tonight?" she exclaimed as she sent a request for a new password... "Finally!" she exclaimed as her new password was accepted... "Fuck!"

"What's wrong Mommy?"

"It's gone – it's all gone!"

"Is my homework gone Mommy?"

"No Billy..."

"Can you help me with this?" he asked as he handed her the math homework. She looked it over quickly...

"You did good Billy – you only missed this..." she said as she pointed out his mistake...

"Oh shoot – I forgot – thank you Mommy..."

"You're welcome..."

"What's the password?"

"Huh?"

"What's the password to Billy's computer?"

"I'll give you a hint..." I answered as I walked over to him and pulled him into a kiss...

"Mmm... is it Kissme?"

"Yea..."

"All caps?" he breathed as he kissed me again...

"Capital K... small i... small s... small s... Capital M... small e... 2... 4..."

"Mmm... KissMe24..."

"Yes..."

"I like that..."

"I have a surprise for you..."

"Is this surprise really for me?"

"Yes..."

"Mmm... when do I get it?"

"It starts tonight..."

"I like the sound of that..."

"Let's get the computer set up and then we can go back downstairs..."

"Okay..." I watched William set up the computer and then he turned it on... "Nice..."

"Thank you for buying it for me..."

"You're welcome..."

"Go on downstairs — I'll be down in a minute..."

"Okay..." I waited for him to go downstairs and then I put a password on my new computer: Gotcha!24...

"Ummm... I think I left something in your office — do you mind if I go upstairs and take a look?" Dawn asked...

"Dawn — I don't think..." William started to say...

"That's fine..." I interrupted. William was more surprised than she was...

"Thanks!" she exclaimed as she hurried upstairs. I waited until she got upstairs and then I went up... "Shit! Where the fuck is it?!"

"Where the fuck is what?" I asked as I walked in...

"Nothing – I must've left it at home..."

"It must be important – I hope you find it..." Dawn didn't respond – she just went back downstairs in a hurry. I smiled to myself and thought of my new password...

"Mommy – I'm hungry..."

"It's too late to cook – Honey – is it okay if I order Chinese?"

"That's fine..."

"That'll take about 45 minutes to get here..." Dawn said...

"You'll be home in less than 45 minutes – unless you're still helping Billy with homework..."

"I'm finished with my homework!" Billy exclaimed...

"That's good – say good night to your mother Billy..."

"Good night Mommy..."

"Good night Billy – I'll see you tomorrow..."

"Good night Dawn..." I said as she opened the door and left...

"I'll order the food now..." I said as I took out my phone...

"I want chicken-fried rice!" Billy exclaimed...

"I'll have black pepper steak cubes with vegetables..." William said...

"I'm having pad thai noodles with chicken & shrimp..." I said as I placed the order. William took out his phone and began reading a text from Dawn...

"What the fuck!"

"What?"

"Did you know she was moving Billy's room downstairs?!"

"No..."

"We agreed he'd stay upstairs! How could you let her do that?!"

"Let her? What do you mean let her?"

"I don't want Billy's room downstairs! She just put him out of his room and you're okay with it!"

"Actually – you're right – I'm okay with it. Moving Billy's room had nothing to do with him – it was about you."

"Me?!"

"Yes – she doesn't want you anywhere near our bedroom."

"You don't have a problem with me being near your bedroom when you wanna fuck me."

"You're right – but I only fuck you when she's not here."

"So you're okay with Billy having access to the front door?"

"Billy will be fine – besides – it needs to be this way so she doesn't figure out we're still fucking."

"Food's here!" I exclaimed as I went to the door, got the bag, and came back inside...

"Yea!" Billy exclaimed as he skipped into the kitchen...

"I know that bitch did something!" she exclaimed as she stormed inside...

"Hey Dawn – what's wrong?"

"When we were married, we agreed that Billy should be upstairs – Demi moved his room downstairs..."

"What's wrong with that?"

"I've never been comfortable with children being so close to the front door – they can walk out or someone can break in and they'd be vulnerable..."

"So you'd rather Billy be upstairs for his own protection?"

"Yes!"

"I'm sure William wouldn't put his son in harm's way..."

"He didn't even know about it!"

"Is he upset?"

"No..."

"Why are you upset then?"

"I guess you're right..." she sighed...

"Did you eat?"

"No – and I'm starving..."

"I ordered Chinese – come sit down with me – we'll have dinner... we'll have some wine... and then we'll have dessert..." he said as he smiled at her mischievously...

"That sounds good..."

"Now... about my surprise..." he breathed in my ear...

"I was thinking..." I said as I turned around...

"Tell me..." he breathed as he kissed me...

"About last night..."

"Go on..."

"The way you fucked me..."

"Go on..." he breathed as he kissed me again...

"Now that the office is upstairs..."

"Yeess..."

"You can bend me over the desk..."

"Yeess..."

"Whenever you want..."

"Yeess..."

"And Billy won't catch us because we can lock the door..."

"Yeess..."

"Mommy?"

"Yes Billy?"

"Can I watch tv?"

"Yes Billy..."

"Okay..."

"What time is it?" I asked...

"It's 8:30 – why?"

"Billy doesn't go to bed until 9..."

"So?"

"So... remember that quickie you wanted this morning?"

"Yeess..."

"Why don't we take advantage of the time we have while Billy's watching tv?"

"Get your ass over here..." he commanded as he started to pull me out the office...

"No... Let's do it here..." I said as I bent over the desk and braced myself. Thank God Billy watches tv with the volume turned up or we would've had some explaining to do...

"What time is it?" I breathed...

"It's 9..."

"Mommy?"

"Yes Billy?"

"Can I come upstairs?"

"Sure you can..."

"What's wrong Billy?" William asked...

"I just wanted to say good night..." he answered as he hugged his father. William was touched by it and he picked Billy up...

"Good night – I love you..."

"I love you too Daddy..."

"Good night Billy..." I said as I took Billy out of William's arms and held him...

"Good night Mommy..."

"I love you..."

"I love you too Mommy..." I put Billy down and he went downstairs...

"I never fucked you in there..."

"I know..."

"Ready for more?"

"I didn't answer him. I went into the bedroom, took off my clothes, and stood there. I knew what was coming and I was ready – but I was just getting started. He had no idea what was coming.

"Good morning... Ooohhh..." he moaned as I sat on his dick...

"Good... morning..." I moaned. William grabbed my ass and pushed himself inside me... "Fuck me..." That sent him into a frenzy...

"You want this dick?!"

"Yes Daddy – Yeesss!" He flipped me over on my back, bent my legs up, and began pounding me...

"Take it!" he growled...

"Fuck me! Yes! Just like that! I'm cumming!"

"Uuugh! Uuugh! Uuugh! Uuugh! Uuugh! Uuuggghhh!" He collapsed on top of me with my legs still pushed up and held them in place as we kissed...

"Mmm... I moaned...

"What's gotten into you?" he breathed...

"You..."

"Mommy?"

"Yes Billy?"

"Can I come in?"

"Just a second..." William answered as he jumped up. He got both our robes, we put them on, and then he opened the door... "What's wrong Billy?"

"Nothing..."

"Come sit with Daddy..." he said as he took Billy by the hand and sat him on the bed. William sat down next to him and put his arm around him... "What's wrong?"

"I like my new room... but..."

"You can tell me Billy..."

"I miss you guys..."

"Aww – you'll get used to it..."

"I guess..."

"Billy?"

"Yes Mommy?"

"You can still come upstairs..."

"I can?"

"Of course..."

"Can I do my homework up here?"

"You need to do your homework downstairs – but you can come up here and keep me company sometimes..."

"Can I come in here with you Daddy?"

"You can come in here sometimes..."

"Okay – I'm going to go downstairs and get ready for school..."

"Okay..."

"I didn't think it would be hard for him to adjust to being away from us..." I sighed...

"He'll be alright... Give it time..."

"I was thinking..."

"Oh?" he asked as he stood up and came over to me...

"Why don't we put in for a personal day?"

"What do you want to do?"

"I want to take Billy to school, I want to come back home, I want to get back in bed, and I want you to give me some more dick..."

"Say less..." he said as he picked up his phone... "Tom... Yea... I need to take a personal day... my wife has an emergency... I'll keep you posted... See you tomorrow..." I smiled at him as I picked up my phone...

"Lisa... I need a personal day... my husband has an emergency... I'll keep you posted... See you tomorrow..."

"Give me your phone..." he commanded. I gave him my phone and he turned it off...

"What about your phone?" He smiled at me, picked his phone up, and turned it off. He watched me intently as I got dressed. I went over to him, pulled him into a kiss, and picked up his phone while I had him distracted... "I'll be back...

"I'll be waiting..."

"You won't be cheating on me today..." I mumbled as I went downstairs...

"I'm ready Mommy..."

"Me too – let's go..."

"Why aren't you answering your phone?! I'm going to stop by to see if I can find what I left in the office the other day – I couldn't find it last night – I'll use the key and I'll make sure I reset the alarm when I leave..."

"Honey? I'm home! Hmm – maybe he's in the bathroom..." I said as I went upstairs...

"Get your ass in here!" he growled as he pulled me inside. He didn't have to tell me to take off my clothes... "Come get this dick..." he commanded as he got on the bed and stretched out. I went over to the bed and climbed on his dick. I forgot I had his phone in my pocket...

"Damn – he's still not answering! Oh well – I'll just let myself in..." she said as she used her key to unlock the door. She put in the pin and turned off the alarm... "I'll look in Billy's new room first..." she said as she went inside...

"You want this dick – right?!"
"Yes Daddy! Yes!"
"Tell me to fuck you..."
"Fuck me! Yes!"

"Dammit – there's nothing in here – it has to be upstairs..." she said as she went upstairs...

"William – stop..."
"You mean don't stop..."
"No – I mean stop..."
"Why the fuck do you want me to stop?!"

"Somebody's here..."

"There's nobody here..."

"Listen!" William went to the door and listened. He came back over towards me, put on his robe, and reached in the nightstand drawer for his gun...

"William... Be careful..."

"Stay here..." he whispered as he went into the hallway. I put my robe on and slid down the side of the bed. I was scared until I heard her scream...

"What the fuck are you doing here?!" he exclaimed...

"You wouldn't answer your phone!"

"What the fuck are you doing here?!" I exclaimed...

"I know I left something here – I came back to..."

"How the fuck did you get in here?!" I interrupted...

"I... I have a key..."

"Why the fuck do you still have a key to this house?!"

"Demi – calm down..."

"NO I WILL NOT! GET THE FUCK OUT OF MY HOUSE!" Dawn didn't move fast enough for me so I charged towards her...

"Demi – No..."

"I'll leave..." she said as she got up and went downstairs...

"LET GO OF ME!" I screamed as I pulled away from him...

"Demi – wait..."

"BITCH – I SAID GET THE FUCK OUT OF MY HOUSE!" Dawn flung the door open and ran out before William could get downstairs...

"DEMI!"

"DON'T YOU FUCKIN' TOUCH ME!" William grabbed me in a bear hug and I couldn't move... "LET GO OF ME!"

"I'm not going to let you go until you calm down..."

"Why was she here?! I exclaimed as I started crying...

"I can explain... but you need to calm down... okay?"

"Okay..."

"I'm going to let you go now..."

"Okay..." William let me go and I was still enraged... "Why was she here?!"

"I don't know..."

"How did she get in?"

"She has a key..."

"Why does she have a key?"

"When we were married, we both had keys. After we got divorced, I told her to keep the key in case she needed to get to Billy in an emergency..."

"I understand that..."

"You do?"

"Yes..."

"Thank God..." he breathed...

"But that doesn't explain what she was doing here – Billy's in school..."

"You're right – and I'm going to get to the bottom of it – where's my phone?"

"It's in my pocket..."

"Upstairs?"

"Yes..."

"Why did you take my phone?"

"I wanted to make sure you weren't called back into work..." William went upstairs to get his phone out my pocket. When he turned it on, he saw all the text messages from earlier, plus a few new ones...

"What the fuck is wrong with your wife?! Is she crazy?! Why aren't you answering your phone?! I sent you messages and you didn't reply!"

"What the fuck is wrong with you?! Why would you just drop by like that?! You should've known not to come over if I didn't answer the phone! What was so fucking important that you decided to risk everything after what happened when she went ballistic because you were in the bedroom?!"

"I lost everything! All my documents! All my emails! Everything!"

"Why the fuck was all that shit on my computer anyway?! Don't you have your own computer?!"

"I'm there every day helping Billy with his homework – I'm on the computer anyway – I didn't think it was a problem!"

"You know what – I should'a let my wife drag your ass!"

"Don't threaten me William!"

"Fuck you!"

"Honey? Is everything alright? Did you find your phone?"

"I found my phone – I'm coming downstairs..." I waited for him to come into the kitchen...

"I have a headache..."

"I'll make you some coffee..."

"All I wanted was for us to spend the day in bed..." I sighed as I started crying...

"Don't cry – I'll call a locksmith – we'll get the locks changed – it won't happen again – I promise..." he said as he came over to me and pulled me into a hug. The kettle started to whistle and he let me go so he could make me coffee. I took my phone out of my pocket...

"Hello? Yes... Could you come by today? You can be here within the hour? Yes... Mrs. Taylor... 246 Court Avenue, Milford, CT... Uh Huh... Okay... Thank you..."

"I'll make breakfast..." I didn't acknowledge I heard him. I just continued to sit there. I didn't speak until he put the cup of coffee on the table...

"Thank you..."

"You're welcome..." I watched him make scrambled eggs with cheese, sausage, potatoes with onions & peppers, and grits. Normally I'd be happy because it's one of my favorite meals but not today... "Here you go..." he said as he put the plate down in front of me...

"Thank you..."

"You're welcome. We ate without speaking and when I was finished, I went to get up...

"Sit – I'll get it..."

"I think the locksmith is here..." I sighed as I went to open the door...

"Good afternoon – are you Mrs. Taylor?"

"Yes – this is my husband, William..."

"Did you have a break in?"

"No – nothing like that – we had a family member living here and they didn't return the key..."

"Okay – we can change the cylinder if you like this design..."

"What do you think Honey?"

"I like the design we have..."

"Do you have any other locks that need to be changed?"

"Yes – the lock on the back door..." William answered. I got up, went to sit on the couch, and took out my phone while the locksmith had William's attention...

"I'm fuckin' livid!"

"What happened?!"

"Dawn happened!"

"Oh no! What did she do?!"

"She let herself in using the key, she turned off the alarm, and she was up in my office looking for her manuscript while we were in the bedroom!"

"WHAT?!"

"We were in bed – William got his gun – she's lucky he didn't shoot her ass!"

"Are you sure William didn't know she was coming over?"

"No – I had his phone."

"How's William?"

"He's angry too."

"Is he mad at you?"

"No."

"Are you okay?"

"No"

"I'm so sorry"

"The locksmith is here."

"You're changing the locks?"

"Yes."

"Good."

"I wanted to hurt her."

"I'm glad you didn't."

"I would've if William didn't stop me."

"I'm glad he stopped you."

"I'm kinda glad too – it would've been bad for Billy."

"I'm going to suggest she leave you alone for the rest of the week."

"I'd love that – but I don't want you to say anything."

"I'll get her to tell me what happened – this way I can bring it up."

"Okay."

"Why'd she still have a key anyway?"

"William said he wanted her to be able to get Billy in an emergency."

"I'm sorry you're going through this."

"I love William – but if I had known this was what it was going to be like..."

"She's coming in – we'll talk soon..."

"Hey Dawn – how was your day?"

"I don't want to talk about it..."

"Hey..." he said as he pulled her into a hug... "What happened?"

"Please... Don't be mad..." she sighed as she sat down. Dante sat down next to her... "I thought I left something in their office last night..."

"Okay..."

"So I tried to call William to let him know I was coming over – but he didn't answer..."

"Okay..."

"I still have a key – for emergencies – so I sent him a text to tell him I was going over there..."

"Did you get a response?"

"No..."

"I'm just going to say this..."

"Here we go..." she sighed as she rolled her eyes...

"You should've waited until tonight when they were home..."

"They were home – he just didn't answer his phone..."

"Maybe he didn't answer his phone because they were busy..."

"Yea – they were busy..."

"Did you call out to let them know you were in the house?"

"No..."

"Dawn!"

"I left something important in there!"

"Do you hear yourself?"

"I shouldn't've told you..."

"There's no getting through to you..." he sighed as he shook his head...

"What's that supposed to mean?"

"Stay away from them for the rest of the week..."

"No I will not – I will go over there and help my son with his homework..."

"Do you love Billy?"

"What kind of question is that?"

"Do you love Billy?"

"Of course I do!"

"Good – then you need to put him first..."

"I always put him first!"

"Prove it – come straight home for the rest of the week – Demi picks Billy up from school anyway – let her help him with his homework for the next couple of days – it'll give Demi a chance to calm down – Billy doesn't need to see tension between the two of you..."

"How do you know Demi was angry?"

"Because if someone came in the house without knocking while we're fucking – I'd be angry..."

"Okay – I'll stay away for today, Thursday, and Friday..."

"Good..." Dawn picked up her phone and sent William a text...

"Hey – I'm sorry about earlier. I'm going to stay away for the rest of the week to give things a chance to calm down. Please tell Billy I'm not feeling well and I'll see him next week."

"I'll give Billy your message. Don't bother trying to use the key again – Demi called a locksmith."

"I'm sorry – Can I come by on Monday and make it up to you?"

"I'll think about it."

"I'll see you Monday – make sure you answer your damn phone! LOL!"

The rest of the week was pure bliss. I was feeling like we were back on our honeymoon. This reset was just what we needed. Billy was so happy I was helping him with his homework he didn't even miss him mother. We were enjoying quickies in the morning and we were going to bed early in the evening. I was feeling so good I started to believe he wasn't cheating on me anymore – I know, I know – let me live for just a second – I said I started to believe – good dick does that – I didn't say I believed – I couldn't believe if I wanted to because it didn't last long...

"Mommy! I missed you!"
"I missed you too!"
"Why the fuck is she here on Saturday?" I sighed as I put on my robe and went downstairs...
"Good morning Mommy..."

"Good morning Billy..."

"I made breakfast..." William said...

"Thank you – Dawn – are you taking Billy out for breakfast?"

"I invited Dawn to have breakfast with us..."

"Why?"

"Why? Why is that even a question?"

"Dawn – why aren't you having breakfast with Dante?'

"I told you before – Dante is none of your business!"

"I'm not trying to get in Dante's business – I'm asking why you don't stay home on the weekends and cook for Dante and invite your son to your house instead of coming over here to have breakfast with my husband..."

"Alright – that's it! I've had enough of this shit! If I want to invite Dawn over to have breakfast with her son – that's what I'll do – and I don't give a fuck if you don't like it!"

"If that's how you feel – enjoy your breakfast!" I exclaimed as I started to storm out the kitchen...

"Get your ass back here and sit the fuck down!" he gritted...

"NO!"

"I SAID GET YOUR ASS BACK IN HERE!" Before I could get away from him he grabbed me and threw me in the chair. Dawn was stunned. Billy was shaking... "EAT IT!" he yelled as he put a plate of food in front of me...

"NO!"

"I SAID EAT IT!" he yelled as he grabbed me in back of my head and shoved my head face down into the plate of food. I struggled to get my hand on the plate because he was too strong. I got my hand on the plate, pushed it out from under me, and it hit the floor. William let go of me to pick up the plate and I jumped up from the chair. I had no idea Billy was right behind me...

"This mutha fucka got the wrong bitch..." I mumbled under my breath as I went upstairs..."

"Mommy?"

"Yes Baby..." I sniffed as I turned around. I had to do something to redeem his father. I saw the tears in his eyes and in that moment I couldn't continue to cry for myself...

"Don't cry Mommy..." he cried as he ran to me and hugged me around my waist...

"I'm okay..." I lied. I hated lying to him...

"No you're not..." he sniffed...

"Billy!" his father bellowed... "Get your ass back down here and finish your breakfast!"

"He'll be down in a minute..." I lied again... "He's in the bathroom..."

"We have a bathroom down here — you know what — that's it — I'm coming upstairs..."

"I'm coming Daddy..." he said as he turned to face his father with a big smile. This poor baby was becoming an expert at lying and it broke my heart...

"Your mother's about to leave..." he said as he turned to go back downstairs...

"Go ahead..." I whispered. Billy looked back at me and hurried back downstairs. I hurried upstairs, ran into the bedroom, and locked the door... "I need to get the fuck outta here..." I huffed as I threw on my clothes. I grabbed my phone, threw it in my purse, and hurried downstairs...

"Where are you going Mommy?"

"Out..." I answered on my way out the door. I jumped in the car, locked the doors, and started the car. William was standing in front of the driveway. I inched as close as I could to avoid hitting him, I turned the steering wheel sharply, and then I stepped on the gas...

"AAAHHH!" he yelled as I ran over the neighbor's fence and sped out his driveway...

"YOU'RE GONNA PAY FOR MY DAMN FENCE!" the neighbor yelled...

"I'm sorry – I'll take care of it..."

"Table for one?" the manager asked...

"Yyyeesss..."

"Are you okay Maam?"

"No..."

"Do you need the police?"

"My friend is on the way..."

"Ana – get her a cup of coffee..." he said as he led me to the booth and helped me sit down...

"Thank you..." I said as I teared up. I took out my phone and called Dante...

"Good morning..."

"Dante..."

"Oh my God – WHAT HAPPENED?!"

"I'm at Galaxy..."

"I'm on my way..." I sat there and sipped the coffee. It was nasty as hell but I was grateful for something. Dante was frantic as he rushed in...

"I'm sorry – I'm looking for..."

"I'm right here..." Dante came over to the table, pulled me up into a hug, and held me...

"Demi... you're shaking..."

"Let's sit down..."

"Your meal is on us – you can order anything you want..." the manager said...

"Thank you – have you had breakfast?"

"Dawn left without cooking..."

"William invited her to breakfast..."

"Why?"

"Because she hasn't seen her son..." I sighed...

"So she can't cook breakfast for me because he invited her to have breakfast with you?!"

"I asked her why she wasn't having breakfast with you and she told me you were none of my business..."

"Thank you for thinking of me – at least somebody is..."

"I'm sorry Dante..."

"Don't worry about me – what happened?'

"William said he was sick of this shit and if he wanted to invite Dawn over to have breakfast with her son that's what he'll do and he doesn't give a fuck if I don't like it..."

"He actually said that to you?"

"Yes..." I sniffed as I teared up. Dante took my hand as the manager came back to the table...

"Have you decided what you want?"

"I like your big breakfast..."

"Make it two..."

"With home fries or grits?"

"Both..." I answered...

"You got it..."

"I told him if that's how you feel – enjoy your breakfast – I tried to leave..."

"Did he hurt you?"

"He threw me in the chair..." I whispered as I teared up...

"I swear to God..."

"He... tried... he grabbed my head..."

"Stop..."

"He pushed my head... into... the... plate..." Dante was red...

"He kept yelling at me to eat... I refused... I pushed the plate on the floor... he bent down to pick up the plate... I ran upstairs... Billy ran after me..."

"Billy?! He was at the table?!"

"Yes..."

"Where was Dawn?"

"She was sitting right there..."

"You need to leave him!"

"He came after Billy – I lied and said Billy was in the bathroom but he knew Billy was checking on me..."

"That poor kid..."

"I ran into the room, locked the door, and threw on my clothes..."

"You don't deserve to live like this..."

"I got in the car... William blocked me from leaving the driveway..."

"Demi?"

"Yes Dante?"

"What did you do?"

"I did what I had to do – I needed to get away from him..."

"Is he alive?' Dante whispered...

"I didn't hit him Dante..."

"Oh thank God..." he breathed... "I turned the steering wheel, I ran over the neighbor's fence, and I drove around him..."

"Here's your breakfast – take your time..."

"Thank you..." we both said...

"What are you going to do?"

"I'm going to eat breakfast..."

"What are you going to do after breakfast?"

"I don't know..."

"Where are you going?" William asked...

"I'm going in my room..."

"Don't be rude – your mother came to see you..."

"Mommy can come..." he said as he left the kitchen...

"I'm sorry..." Dawn sighed...

"You have nothing to be sorry for – I invited you..."

"William – this is bad..."

"Don't start..."

"I've never seen you treat her like that..."

"Billy – come say good bye to your mother!"

Billy hurried out his room...

"Bye Mommy!"

"$\mathcal{H}$ave you made a decision?"

"Yea..." I sighed...

"You're going back to him...

"I have to..."

"I'm going to say this – and you need to hear it..."

"Go ahead..." I sighed...

"You are lying to yourself..."

"That's not true..."

"You just told me you have to go back to him – but the truth is – you want to go back to him..."

"Dante... you don't understand..."

"Oh I understand perfectly – you're the one that's confused..."

"I'm not confused... I..."

"You keep hoping he'll change..."

"Yes..."

"You love him – I get that – but you need to love yourself..."

"I do love myself..."

"If you really loved yourself you'd put yourself first and walk away..."

"I can't just walk away..."

"There you go lying to yourself again..."

"Dante..."

"Come take a ride with me..."

"I can't – what if..."

"You can..." he breathed as he pulled me into a kiss... "And you will..."

"Dante... what if Dawn..."

"Fuck her..."

"Dante... I want to... but..."

"Did you just say you want to?"

"Yes..." Dante took my hand and led me out the restaurant... "What about my car?"

"Leave it..." I got in the car with him and left my car in the parking lot...

"Hmm..." William mumbled... "You've been at Galaxy for a while – Billy!"

"Yes Daddy?"

"Get your coat – we're going to look for Mommy..."

"Where are we?"

"We're in Darien..." I knew Darien was beautiful but now that I was seeing it at this pace, I really appreciated the beauty of Darien.

Dante took my hand and squeezed it as I continued to look out the window...

"Good afternoon – table for two?" the manager greeted...

"I'm looking for my wife..." William answered as he took out his phone and showed him a picture of me...

"Oh yes – she was here..."

"Was?"

"She left about an hour ago..."

"Was she alone?"

"She came in alone..."

"Are you sure she was alone?"

"Yes sir – why do you ask?"

"Because my wife's car is still in the parking lot..."

"Maybe she took an Uber..."

"Hmmm – I didn't think of that – thank you..."

"You're welcome..." William said as he took Billy's hand and left...

"She's in trouble..." Ana said...

"I'm afraid so..." the manager confirmed...

"Dante..."

"I know..." he sighed as he turned the car around... "I'll take you back to the diner..." We rode back in silence. I had no idea how I was going to explain this to William but at the same time, I didn't care. When Dante kissed me it changed everything... "Penny for your thoughts?"

"I'm thinking about you..."

"Me?"

"Yes... You..."

"Wow..."

"Why did you kiss me?"

"Because I wanted to..." We continued to ride and I started to get sad when I got back to the diner... "Oh no..." Dante said as the manager came running to the car. Dante rolled down the window... "What's wrong?"

"Her husband - he was here – with their son..."

"What did you tell him?"

"I told him she came in alone..."

"Thank you..."

"Miss – are you going to be okay?"

"I'll be okay..."

"You come back and see me if you need to..."

"Thank you – I will..." I said as the manager turned to go back inside...

"Come here..." Dante breathed as he tried to pull me into a kiss again...

"Dante... No... I can't..."

"Okay..."

"I'll call you..." I said as I got out the car. Dante drove off and I got in my car. I still wasn't ready to go home so I headed towards Trumbull Mall..."

"Where the hell have you been?!" Dawn snapped...

"Who the fuck do you think you're talking to?!"

"You – where the hell have you been?!"

"Where the hell were you?"

"I was invited to have breakfast with my son..."

"So – you got up early this morning – you left me here – to go have breakfast with William?! Let me ask you something – why couldn't you tell me you want us to go out to breakfast and we pick your son up and take him out – bad enough you're there every night as it is – and when you do come home you never offer to cook me something to eat – but you make sure your ass eats – with him!"

"You're jealous..."

"You're so deluded you didn't even hear what I just said!"

"You know it's about my son – it has nothing to do with William!"

"It has everything to do with him – you never got over him – that's why you jump every time he snaps his finger!"

"Oh my God! You're jealous of my child too?!"

"Please miss me with the bullshit. These last couple of days reminded me of why I fell in love with you in the first place..."

"Oh Dante..."

"Save it – it didn't last long – it never does – let me tell you something – I'm not going to be the other man in your life – either I'm going to be the only man in your life – or I'm gone!"

"Dante – I'm sorry – I'll do better – you're right – I don't need to be there every night – I'm sorry I didn't cook you breakfast – did you eat?"

"Are you fuckin' kidding me?! I've been gone all day – your phone isn't broke – if you gave a damn about me I would've heard from you!" Dawn got up and went over to him...

"I'm sorry Baby... I... things didn't go well..."

"Billy wasn't happy to see you?"

"He was... but Demi wasn't..."

"You wanna talk about it?" Dawn responded by pulling him into a kiss. Dante picked her up in his arms and took her into the bedroom.

"*H*mmm... she's at Trumbull Mall..."

William sighed...

"Daddy?"

"Yes Billy?"

"Where's Mommy?"

"Mommy's out shopping..."

"Is she coming home?"

"Yes Billy..."

"Excuse me..."

"Yes?"

"Could you help me find an air mattress?"

"Sure – what size were you looking for?"

"Queen..."

"How 'bout this one?" she asked as she showed me the Sound Sleep Dream Series Luxury Air Mattress with Comfort Coil Technology & Built-in-High Capacity Pump..."

"I'll take it..."

"Okay..." she said as she took it down from the shelf..."

"Thank you..."

"You're welcome..."

"Mommy!" Billy exclaimed as he nearly knocked me down...

"Hello Billy..." I laughed...

"Hello Demi..." I didn't respond...

"What did you buy Mommy?"

"Something for the office..." I answered as I headed upstairs. William followed me...

"Can we talk?"

"No..." I answered as I went into the office, closed the door, and locked it. I sat down at the desk, turned on the computer, and heard a key in the lock... "What are you doing in here?"

"I need to talk to you..."

"Leave me alone William..."

"Please..." he whispered. I turned around and he was crying... "I'm sorry..." I got up from the chair and ran to him... "I'm sorry..." he breathed as he kissed me...

"William... Stop..."

"Why?"

"Because... I need... time..."

"Time? Time for what?"

"I need time to forgive you..."

"Fine..." he sighed as he turned to leave and left. I wanted to forgive him but I couldn't.

Sorry wasn't enough.   I thought about what Dante said to me as I set up the mattress...

"Mommy?"
"Yes Billy?"
"Do you wanna play my game with me?"
"Sure..." I answered as I went downstairs...
"I'm making dinner..." I didn't respond. I went inside, sat down with Billy, and we started a game...

"Bitch thinks I don't know what she's up to..." he mumbled under his breath... "She got another thing coming if she thinks I'm letting her go... Even if she wants a divorce – she'll be back – just like Dawn – she needs time to forgive me – if anything – I need time to forgive her – this is all her fault anyway – all she had to do was sit the fuck down and eat – but no – she had to make a big deal out of nothing – now I gotta jump through fuckin' hoops to get her to forgive me – she's lucky I love her – I'll just keep fuckin' Dawn until she's ready to forgive me and give me some pussy..."

"Dinner's ready..." he said as he opened Billy's door...
"Coming Daddy..." I got up and followed Billy into the kitchen... "It smells good Daddy..." William put two plates on the table and then he went to make a plate for himself...
"Why aren't you eating?"

"We're waiting for you..." I answered. William smiled as he sat down...

"Jasmine rice..." I said...

"Yes..."

"What's Jasmine rice?" Billy asked...

"It's one of Mommy's favorites..." William answered...

"Thank you..." I said...

"You're welcome." We sat there eating Jasmine rice with teriyaki chicken and mixed vegetables. William knew what he was doing...

"Can I take a juice and go in my room?"

"Yes Billy..." William answered...

"Okay!" William looked at me and waited for Billy to close his bedroom door...

"Can we talk?"

"Sure..."

"I'm sorry..."

"You said that..."

"I should've discussed it with you..."

"Absolutely..."

"I'm trying to do what's best for Billy but you're not helping the situation..."

"I'm done..." I said as I started to get up...

"Demi wait – please..." I sat back down... "I came downstairs to make breakfast..."

"I know that..."

"I went to wake Billy up and he was crying..."

"Oh no..."

"I asked him why he was crying and he told me he missed his mother..."

"Oh my God... Why didn't you tell me?"

"I didn't get a chance to tell you – you came downstairs – you over-reacted... and..."

"You are so full of shit..."

"I told you – Billy was crying..."

"If you had time to call her and invite her to breakfast – you had time to tell me Billy was crying, he missed his mother, or whatever – like you said – you did what you wanted to do and you didn't give a damn whether I like it or not..."

"Keep your voice down!"

"Why – are you going to shove my head into this plate too?"

"I'm done..." he sighed as he got up..."

"Thanks for dinner!" I snapped. William went upstairs and I went to check on Billy. I opened the door and he'd fallen asleep. I turned off the tv and the light, closed the door, and went into the bathroom. I looked in the mirror and saw a bruise on the top of my head... "Dammit – I was riding around with this bruise on my head all day?" I sighed as I lifted my head and checked my neck for bruises...

"I'm going to bed..."

"Good night..." I said as I kept looking at myself in the mirror...

"What are you doing?"

"I'm looking for bruises..." He left me alone and went upstairs. When I got upstairs, I went into the office and locked the door. I put the chair under the lock and went to lie down on the air mattress...

"Open the door..."

"No..."

"Open the door Demi..."

"Go to bed William..." I sighed as I turned over on my side and went to sleep.

*I*t was Friday morning... "Demi..."

"I'm up." I got up, stretched, and got up off the mattress. I moved the chair out from under the lock and opened the door... "William..." Before I could say anything else, he pulled me into a kiss and kissed me hard...

"William... I..."

"Sshh..." he whispered as he put a finger over my lips. He took me by the hand, led me into the bedroom, and locked the door...

"William..." I breathed as he kissed me again...

"Don't..."

"Please..."

"Fine..." he sighed as he pulled away from me...

"I forgive you..." He just stood there... "Did you hear me?"

"I heard you..." he answered as he smiled at me mischievously...

"I need to..."

"You need to let me make love to you..." he interrupted...

"Yes... I do..."

"Stay here..." he commanded. I didn't move. He left me in the room as he went downstairs...

"Mommy!" I heard Billy exclaim...

"Good morning Billy..."

"You're early..."

"I'm here to take you to school..."

"Yeeaaa!"

"Thank you Dawn..."

"Thank you..." I heard her say as she closed the door. I got anxious as I listened to his footsteps. He came back in the bedroom and he had a look on his face I hadn't seen since our wedding night. I knew he was up to something but I wasn't sure what...

"Did you miss me?" he breathed as he pulled me into a kiss...

"Yes..."

"Let me see how much..." he growled as he put his hand between my legs and pushed his fingers inside...

"Huh..." I moaned...

"Yea... you missed me..." he breathed as he picked me up in his arms and carried me to the bed...

"William..." I whispered as he stood in front of me and began stroking his dick...

"You want this?"

"Yes..."

"Say it...

"I want it..."

"Beg me..."

"What?"

"You heard me..." he growled as he continued stroking his dick...

"Please..."

"Please what?"

"Please fuck me..." He got on the bed, pushed my legs apart, bent my knees up, and pushed the tip in...

"Yesss..." I moaned...

"No..." he said as he got up off me and stood up...

"William... what..."

"Get dressed – you're going to be late for work..." he said as he went in the bathroom and locked the door. I got my things, went downstairs, and turned on the shower...

"Mutha fucka..." I mumbled as I put soap on the loofah and began to wash myself. When I got to my pussy, I slowed down... "Ooohhh..." I moaned as the loofah went over my clit. I pushed my fingers up inside me, closed my eyes, and imagined Dante kissing me again... "Dante...

Dante... Dante..." I whispered as I started cumming...

"That's what the fuck you get..." he laughed as he washed himself. When he got to his dick he slowed down... "Don't worry – Dawn's on her way back – You'll get some pussy in a few..."

I got out the shower, toweled off, got dressed, and came out the bathroom...
"I'll see you tonight..."
"See you tonight..." I said as I left. I got in the car, put on my seat belt, started the car, and connected my phone to the speaker...

"Good morning..."
"Hey..."
"I'm on my way to work..."
"I haven't heard from you..."
"I know..."
"Are you okay?"
"Yea..."
"What happened when you got home?"
"Nothing..."
"Nothing?"
"I went to the mall and bought an air mattress..."
"Oohhh..."
"He made dinner..."
"Did he ask you where you were?"
"No..."

"So you had dinner..."

"If you can call it that..."

"What happened?"

"He wanted to talk so I agreed. He told me he invited Dawn over because Billy was crying and told him he missed his mother..."

"Bullshit..."

"Exactly..."

"He could've told you that..."

"He claimed he didn't have a chance to tell me that because I over-reacted..."

"Unbelievable!"

"He had the nerve to tell me he was doing his best to co-parent but I wasn't helping the situation!"

"Oh my God – you know something – this is one of the worst cases of narcissism I've ever heard!"

"I started thinking I was crazy..."

"Don't you dare!"

"I know – I'm not..."

"How dare he turn this on you!"

"I told him he did what he wanted to do and he didn't give a fuck if I liked it or not..."

"Damn right!"

"He told me to keep my voice down and I asked him why – are you going to push my head in this plate of food too?"

"Damn Demi – I'm sorry – did he ever apologize?"

"He did..."

"Did you accept his apology?"

"I told him I needed time to forgive him..."

"Good for you..."

"I've been sleeping in my office since Sunday..."

"Oh wow – you were serious..."

"Yea..."

"Was that hard?"

"Not really... I was able to sleep but I missed him..."

"I guess I can understand that..."

"Thank you..."

"For what?"

"For not calling me a fool..."

"I would never call you that..."

"I have something to tell you..."

"Oh yea?"

"I haven't stopped thinking about what happened between us..."

"Interesting..."

"Interesting? That's all you have to say?"

"I'm more interested in what you have to say..."

"I don't understand..."

"Don't bullshit me Demi..."

"Why would you say that to me?!"

"You can't stop thinking about what happened between us because you wanted it to happen..."

"That's not true..."

"So... you didn't want me to kiss you?"

"No..."

"Why didn't you push me away then?"

"I didn't push you away because..."

"Say it Demi..."

"It felt good..."

"There. Was that so hard?"

"Yes..."

"Why?"

"I'm married!"

"So what?"

"Dante!"

"You were hurting – you needed to be comforted – that's why you called me..."

"Yes... but..."

"Don't beat yourself up about it – you didn't kiss me – I kissed you..."

"Okay..."

"Can I see you?"

"No..."

"Why?'

"Dante... I can't..."

"Come by tonight after work..."

"I can't... they'll be waiting for me..."

"It won't be long... I just wanna see you..."

"Okay..."

"I'll see you tonight..."

"Hey..." Dawn sighed. William pulled her into a kiss and kissed her hard...

"Damn – what brought that on?"

"I need pussy..." he answered as he took her by the hand and pulled her towards Billy's room...

"William... No... Not in here!"

"Why not?!"

"This is Billy's room!"

"Get your ass on the bed..." he laughed as he pushed her down...

"I can't believe you're about to fuck me on our son's bed..." she breathed as he got on top of her. William responded by pulling her clothes down...

"Wait a minute..." she laughed...

"I'm tired of waiting... I need pussy... and I need it now..." he growled as he thrust himself inside her...

"Oh shit – Yes – Fuck me..."

"Gimme that pussy..."

"Huh... Huh... Huh... Huh..."

"Uuugh! Uuugh! Uuugh! Uuugh!"

"Don't stop... Right there... Harder... Fuck... I'm cumming!"

"Uuugh! Uuugh! Uuugh! Uuugh! Uuuggghhh!" William collapsed on top of her and began kissing her...

"Damn Baby – you just fucked the shit outta me..."

"You want more?"

"Hell yea..."

"Say less..." he growled as he started pounding her...

"HAAH! HAAH! HAAH! HAAH!"

"Uuugh! Uuugh! Uuugh! Uuugh!"

"FUCK ME! I'M CUMMING AGAIN! AAAHHH!"

"UUUGGGHHH!" Damn that was good..." he laughed...

"How long as it been?"

"A week..."

"Damn – if you're gonna fuck me like that – I hope she never gives you pussy again!"

"She'll give me some pussy soon – she'll give me some pussy tonight..."

"What makes you so sure?"

"I left her hanging this morning..."

"Damn William – that's fucked up..."

"That'll teach her a lesson..."

"That's just gonna piss her off..."

"Naa – she's horny as fuck – and when she comes home – I'm gonna fuck the shit outta her and remind her whose pussy that is..."

"Damn William – you're a cocky mutha fucka..."

"Fuck you talkin' about – you may be fuckin' Dante – but your pussy is mine too..."

"I know..."

"So – you admit it?"

"Yes..."

"Damn right it is..." he gritted as he pushed her down on her back...

I could barely concentrate. I kept replaying the conversation we had over and over. I was feeling guilty because he made me feel good. I was feeling guilty because I admitted it... "Why are you beating yourself up like this?" I sighed. I couldn't wait to get off work...

"Hey..."

"Hey..." I sighed...

"It's good to see you..."

"It's good to see you too..." Dante pulled me into a hug and kissed me...

"Dante... No..."

"Let me make you feel good..."

"Dante... I can't... I can't..."

"You want to..."

"Yes... I want to... but..."

"It's okay... We don't have to... Mmm..." Why did this man feel so fucking good?

"Dante... I need to go..."

"Stop kissing me back then..."

"Let go of me..."

"I'm not stopping you..."

"I need to go..." I said as I got up. Dante looked at me and smiled mischievously as I left.

"*H*i Mommy..." Billy greeted...

"Hi Billy – Hello Dawn..."

"Hello..." I went over to William and pulled him into a kiss...

"I'll get started on dinner..." I said as I went into the kitchen...

"Mommy – are you coming?"

"Yes Billy..." she answered as she got up and went into his room...

"Hey..." he breathed into my ear as he pulled me to him from behind...

"Hey... that tickles..."

"I'm going to fuck the shit outta you tonight..."

"Promise?"

"Promise..." I smiled to myself as he went back into the living room... "Smells good..."

"Thank you..."

"Honey?"

"Yes?"

"Did Dawn ever find what she was looking for the other day?"

"Why are you asking me that?"

"Never mind..."

"What are you cooking?"

"Cheeseburgers & fries..."

"Why the fuck did she ask me that?" he mumbled...

"I'm heading out..." Dawn said as she came into the living room...

"Finished already?" I asked...

"Billy didn't have that much homework..."

"I'm finished Mommy..." Billy added...

"That's good – hey Dawn – did you ever find what you were looking for the other day?"

"No – why are you asking?"

"You seemed upset – it must've been important..."

"It was..."

"Hopefully it'll turn up..."

"Hopefully – anyway – I need to get going – you ready Billy?"

"Ready? Ready for what?"

"William – you didn't tell her?"

"Tell me what?"

"I'm taking Billy for the weekend – he'll be back on Sunday..."

"Oh wow – that's nice –you must be happy Billy..."

"I am Mommy..."

"Come give me a hug..."

"Okay!" Billy ran to me and gave me a hug... "Bye Mommy!"

"Bye – I'll see you Sunday." I didn't speak until they left... "Thank you..." I sighed...

"You're welcome..."

"I can't believe we have the house to ourselves..."

"Neither can I..."

"Dinner's ready." William came into the kitchen...

"You made a plate for Billy..."

"I thought he was going to be here..."

"Don't worry about it – we'll eat it..." he said as he sat down...

"Hey Babe..." Dawn greeted as she walked in with Billy...

"Hey – Hey Billy! Are you staying for the weekend?'

"Yes!"

"C'mon – I'll take you to the guest room..."

"I'll make dinner..."

"It's Friday – order pizza..."

"Yeaa!" Billy exclaimed...

"I'll be there in a minute..."

"Take your time – I wanna talk to Billy..."

"Okay..."

"Am I in trouble?'

"Why would you be in trouble?'

"I dunno..."

"Relax —I haven't seen you in a while — I just wanna talk..."

"Okay..."

"So... how've you been?"

"I'm okay..."

"You like school?"

"Yea..."

"I heard you have a new room..."

"How did you know?"

"Your mother told me..."

"Oh..."

"Do you like it?"

"It's nice... but..."

"What's wrong?"

"I don't wanna get in trouble..."

"You won't get in trouble Billy — I promise..."

"I wanna go back upstairs..."

"Why?"

"I miss them..."

"Did you tell them that?"

"Yea..."

"What did they say?"

"Mommy said I can still come upstairs..."

"Well that's good..."

"Don't tell Mommy..."

"Why?"

"Mommy and Demi will fight..."

"I won't tell them — but you don't have to worry — they won't fight..."

"Demi got mad at Mommy... and Daddy hit her..."

"I'm so sorry..." he sighed as he hugged Billy...

"Don't tell – I'll get in trouble..."

"I won't tell – I promise..."

"I just want us to be a happy family..."

"I know you do..."

"It's Mommy's fault..."

"What's Mommy's fault?"

"Mommy was in the room with Daddy... Demi got mad..."

"Demi's not mad at you..."

"I know... but she's mad at Mommy – that's why she moved my room downstairs..."

"I'm sorry Billy..."

"Daddy says I'll get used to it..."

"You will..."

"I wish I lived here..."

"You do?"

"Yea..."

"You don't like living with your father?"

"I love Daddy... but if I lived here they wouldn't fight... and my room wouldn't be downstairs..."

"Pizza's here!"

"C'mon – let's go eat..."

"You won't tell – right?"

"I won't tell – I promise..." Billy ran out the guest room and Dante took out his phone..."

"We need to talk about Billy ASAP!"

"We need to talk..."

"Can we fuck?"

"You wanna fuck?"

"Yes..." William got up from the table and stood in front of me...

"Get up..." I stood up... "Get your ass upstairs..." I hurried upstairs and he followed behind me... "Take off your clothes..." I took my clothes off and stood there... "Get your ass in the bed..." I got in the bed on my hands and knees... "Is that how you want it?"

"Yes..." William came up behind me and grabbed my hips... "William... Please..."

"Yes... that's it... beg me..."

"Please fuck me..." William understood the assignment. We spent the next hour fucking in so many positions I lost count. If I knew this was all it took, I would've denied him pussy sooner...

"Good morning..." I yawned...

"Good morning..."

"I smell coffee..."

"I made breakfast..."

"I'll be right down..." I said as I got up...

"See you downstairs..." he said as he left. I went to the bathroom, put my robe on, picked up my phone, and turned it on... "Hmmm..." I said as I saw the message from Dante... "His mother is there – she can take care of him..." I said as I turned my phone off, put it on the nightstand, and went downstairs...

"You said you'd be right down..."

"I went to the bathroom..."

"We need to talk..."

"Okay..." I sighed...

"I'm sorry..."

"You said that..."

"I'm not just saying it..."

"Okay..."

"I went too far..."

"You did..."

"I ran you out of the house..."

"You did..."

"I never meant to hurt you Demi..."

"I believe you..."

"You do?"

"Yes..."

"Do you still love me?"

"Yes..."

"Say it..."

"I love you William..."

"I love you too..."

"I'm sorry about Neil's fence..."

"I took care of it..."

"Can we go back upstairs?"

"You wanna go back upstairs?"

"Yes..."

"We can go back upstairs... but I'm not done talking..."

"Okay..."

"Where were you on Saturday?"

"I went to Darien..."

"Billy asked for you..."

"Aww..."

"He asked me if you were coming back home..."

"I needed..."

"You don't have to explain – I get it..."

"You do?"

"Of course I do..." he said as he stood up and came over to me... "Billy made me realize I need to be better – I need to do better..." he said as he pulled me up into a kiss...

"William..." I sighed...

"That's why I called Dawn and asked her to take Billy for the weekend..."

"Can we go back upstairs now?"

"Yes..." William took my hand, led me upstairs, and fucked me to sleep...

"Demi..."

"Huh?"

"Come with me..." I got up and followed him into the bathroom...

"William..." I whispered as I teared up. He dimmed the lights and I was in awe. The tea tree candles spelled out 'I Love You' as they floated on top of the bubbles. William took me by the hand and helped me into the spa tub. The water splashed all over the tea tree candles but it didn't matter because there were candles all over the bathroom. He slid down in the tub, leaned back, and motioned for me to come to him. I straddled his dick, he grabbed me by my hips, and we began bucking wildly...

"Damn..." I laughed...

"What's so funny?"

"We got water all over the floor..."

"That's what towels are for..." he said as he got out the tub. I got out the tub and started to get some towels... "I got it – go get in bed – I'll be there in a minute..."

"Okay..." I got in bed and waited. William came out the bathroom and stood there looking at me...

"You want more?"

"Yes please..."

"Well..." he said as he got in bed beside me... "Since you asked me so nicely..." he said as he got on top of me..."

"Honey?" I called out. It was dark so I sat up... "Hmmm – smells good..." I said as I got up, put on my robe, and went downstairs...

"You're up..."

"Yea..."

"I made dinner..."

"Thank you..." I sighed as I sat down. William put salad, garlic bread sticks, and Fettucine Alfredo on the table... "Honey?"

"Yes Demi?"

"Can Dawn take Billy every weekend?"

"We can talk about it..." he answered as he made our plates.

 $\mathscr{I}$ t was Monday morning. I was still high from the weekend. I started the car and connected my phone... "Good morning..." I answered...

"How was your weekend?"

"It was wonderful..."

"Sorry to hear that..."

"Dante!"

"I'm just playin' – did you get my message?"

"Yes..."

"Billy's not happy..."

"He seems happy..."

"He's pretending..."

"How do you know?"

"He told me..."

"He told you he's pretending?"

"Billy told me he likes his room but he wants to be back upstairs..."

"I know – I told him he can still come upstairs..."

"That's not it..."

"What is it then?"

"He told me it's his mother's fault you moved his room downstairs..."

"I never told him that!"

"He said his mother was in his father's room – you got mad at his mother ⋅ and that's why you moved his room downstairs..."

"Oh my God..." I whispered as I started crying...

"He also told me you got mad at his mother and his father hit you..."

"I told you about that..."

"Demi – he said he wished he lived with us so you wouldn't fight..."

"What am I gonna do?! She wouldn't stop! Even after I moved his room downstairs – she was still upstairs!"

"Demi – I know..."

"Did he tell his mother?"

"No – I promised him I wouldn't tell – he's afraid of getting in trouble..."

"This is so fucked up – I asked William if Dawn could take Billy every weekend – I thought that would make everybody happy..."

"That's not enough..."

"Why do I have to bend over backwards for that bitch?!"

"Because that's what Billy needs..."

"I'm sorry – I love Billy – but I'm not moving his room back upstairs – and I'm not giving Dawn free reign in my house..."

"I'm not suggesting you do that..."

"What are you suggesting then?"

"Try to be nice to his mother – Billy told me he wishes that we could all be a happy family..."

"I can't believe I have to – you know what – never mind – I'll deal with it..."

"You will?"

"I'll try – especially if she's going to take Billy every weekend..."

"Every weekend?"

"I hope so..."

"I hope not..." Dante mumbled...

"What did you say – I couldn't hear you..."

"Nothing – can I see you later?"

"Not tonight – I need to go straight home..."

"Okay – I'll talk to you later – bye..."

"How was your weekend?"

"It was great..."

"You're welcome..."

"I need to ask you something..."

"Okay..."

"I need you to take Billy every weekend..."

"Nope..."

"Why not?"

"I'm here five nights a week – weekends are my time..."

"What if I want a weekend?"

"You didn't think about that when you took custody..."

"I'm thinking about it now..."

"You're only asking me to do this because you wanna make her happy..."

"Yes – I want to make my wife happy..."

"What about Billy?"

"He'll be spending time with you on the weekends..."

"Dante won't like it..."

"Dante knew you had a child when he got with you..."

"He also knew that you had custody – Dante doesn't want kids – why do you think we don't have any?"

"Look – that's between you and Dante – I wouldn't have to have this conversation with you if you didn't over-step your boundaries..."

"Me?!"

"Yes!"

"You didn't give a damn about boundaries as long as we kept fucking!"

"I still don't – but this isn't going to work if you don't take him on the weekends – I need my wife to be happy..."

"Fuck her..."

"Watch it Dawn..."

"You didn't give a fuck before – why do you give a fuck now?"

"Like you said – you've never seen me treat her like that – she doesn't deserve it..."

"I agree – she doesn't deserve it – but that shouldn't mean I have to give up my weekends..."

"You don't wanna give up your weekends – fine – give up your weeknights..."

"What?!"

"Either you take him on the weekends – or you stop coming over during the week to help him with his homework – Demi can help him with his homework – I can have some peace – and my wife will be happy..."

"So this is all about her..."

"It's about all of us..."

"Bullshit – this is about your wife..."

"It's about Billy too – do you really think it's good for him to see you and Demi arguing?"

"We wouldn't be arguing if she would keep her mouth shut..."

"This is my fault..."

"Finally!"

"I should've checked you the first time you over-stepped your boundaries..."

"Unfuckin'believable!"

"That was my mistake – it won't happen again though – you can take him on the weekends or you can stop coming during the week – what's it going to be?"

"What if I stop giving you pussy?"

"You think that's a threat? Aaahhh Haaaa Haaaa Haaaa! The way Demi put it on me this weekend – I won't miss your pussy!"

"You Bastard!"

"Stop with the dramatics – you can continue to come over every morning – we fuck – you can come over every night – you help Billy with his homework – you take Billy on Friday night – you bring him back on Sunday afternoon – Billy doesn't witness arguing between the two of you – and everybody stays happy..."

"What if I don't?"

"You saw what happened to Demi – right?"

"Fine..."

"Good – now go on – I need to get to work...

"Hey..." I sighed as I came in...

"Mommy!" Billy greeted...

"Hey Billy – Hello Dawn..."

"Hello..."

"Billy – come sit down – we need to talk..." William said...

"Am I in trouble?"

"No Billy..."

"Can I put my stuff in my room?"

"Sure..."

"What would you like for dinner?" I asked...

"Dinner can wait..."

"Yes Daddy?" Billy said as he came to sit down...

"Did you have fun this weekend with your mother?"

"Yes Daddy..."

"Well – your mother and I were talking... and..."

"Billy - I'll be taking you home every Friday..."

"I'm going to spend every weekend with you and Dante?!"

"Yes Baby..."

"Yeeaaa!"

"C'mon – Let's do your homework..."

"Okay!" I waited for them to go in the room and then I pulled William into a kiss so fast it startled him...

"I love you..."

"I love you too – I want steak, scalloped potatoes, and broccoli..."

"Say less!" I exclaimed as I got up. I was so happy. I was even happier when Dawn went home...

"Good night Mommy..."

"Good night Billy..."

"Good night Dawn..." I said...

"Good night..."

"Mommy?"

"Yes Billy?"

"Can I sit in the living room and watch tv with you guys?"

"Sure..." I said as I put the dishes in the dishwasher. William went to sit in the living room and Billy cuddled up next to him. I started the dishwasher and sat down next to them...

"Hey Babe..." Dante greeted as he pulled Dawn into a kiss...

"Hey..." she sighed...

"What's wrong?"

"We need to talk..."

"What happened now?"

"Nothing – it's just..."

"Dawn – what is it?"

"Billy's coming over here every weekend..."

"Every weekend?"

"Yea..."

"Okay..."

"Okay?"

"Sure – he's a good kid – I don't mind him coming over on the weekends..."

"Oh thank God – I thought you'd be upset..."

"Naa..."

"I've had a long day – I'm going to get in the shower – care to join me?"

"I'd love to..."

"I'll meet you in the shower..." she said as she hurried towards their bedroom...

"Hmmph – this mutha fucka thinks he can have his wife, fuck my lady, and have me babysit his kid on the weekends – I'm putting a stop to all this shit – all I want is Demi – and I know just how to get her..."

"Dante! I'm waiting!"

"I'm coming!"

"*D*on't leave me Demi..."

"I have to..."

"You don't have to – you want to – that's the difference between us..."

"Why are you making this so hard?"

"I'm making this hard?! He fuckin' chokes you – he put his hands on you in front of that bitch and their son – and I'm the one that's making this hard?!"

"That's not what I mean..." I sighed as I started crying...

"Come here..." he breathed as he pulled me into a hug and let me cry on his shoulder... "I'm sorry – I know this is hard on you – I wish I could beat his fuckin' ass!"

"I wish you could too..." I sniffed...

"Don't leave me – stay with me... Please..."

"I want to – but I can't – I have to..."

"Pick up that fuckin' kid from school – Yea – I know…" he sighed…

"Dante… he's just a kid… it's not his fault…"

"I know – I'm sorry – that was fucked up – I wish his mother had custody so you didn't have to do his bidding…"

"I'm not doing his bidding…"

"Yes you are…"

"It's not like that…"

"What's it like then?"

"I… I love him…"

"I know that – but I don't understand it…"

"I'm not talking about William – I'm talking about Billy…"

"See – I hate this shit – you went and got attached – that's gonna make it harder for you to leave…"

"I know…"

"Let me ask you something – and I want you to be honest with me…" he said as he picked up my face by my chin…"

"Yes Dante?"

"Do you love me?"

"Dante – how could you ask me that?'

"Answer me… Please…"

"I love you Dante…"

"Say it again…" he breathed as he pulled me into a kiss…

"I… Love… You… Dante…" I breathed as he laid me back on the couch… "Dante…"

"Don't make me stop…"

"Dante… I'm sorry… I can't…"

"Why?!" he asked me as he sat up... "He's fuckin' Dawn so why can't I fuck you?!"

"That's not true – he's fuckin' somebody else..." I answered as I sat up...

"I really didn't want to have to do this..." he sighed as he took out his phone and handed it to me...

"Do what?"

"Look at the text messages from Dawn..." I started to read the messages and I went ballistic... "YOU MEAN TO TELL ME HE'S BEEN FUCKIN' DAWN SINCE WE'VE BEEN MARRIED?!"

"Yes..." he sighed...

"WHY THE FUCK DIDN'T YOU TELL ME?!"

"YOU'RE MAD AT ME?! ARE YOU FUCKIN' SERIOUS RIGHT NOW?!"

"I'M NOT MAD AT YOU – I'M JUST FUCKIN' MAD!!"

"That's why I didn't tell you..."

"Were you ever going to tell me?" I asked with tears in my eyes...

"Uh uh – stop that – you're not crying over that mutha fucka – you hear me?"

"I can't believe him – I knew he was cheating on me – but with her? All the time she comes around – smiling in my face – knowing damn well he treats me like shit – I don't believe I was stupid enough..." Dante interrupted my rant by pulling me into a kiss and kissed me so hard it startled me...

"Damn..." I breathed...

"Make love to me... Please..." he breathed as he kissed me again...

"Dante... I..."

"You don't want me..." he sighed...

"Look at me..." Dante turned his head...

"Look at me..." He looked at me reluctantly...

"Let me call Dawn..."

"Why the fuck..." This time I interrupted him with a kiss...

"I need to call Dawn and tell her I'm stuck in traffic..."

"So..." he breathed as we continued kissing... "You need her to pick up Billy..."

"Yes..."

"What if she asks where you are?"

"She won't..."

"What if William calls you?"

"My battery died... I needed to charge my phone..."

"What if he checks your location?"

"I disabled it before I came over here..."

"Damn... You've thought of everything..." he breathed as he tried to kiss me again...

"Hello Demi..."

"Dawn..." I breathed as Dante kissed my neck...

"Why are you breathing like that?"

"I'm so fuckin' aggravated – I'm stuck in traffic – I won't make it on time to pick up Billy..."

"Fine – I'll go get him..."

"Thank you..."

"You don't have to thank me for picking up my child..."

"Oh shoot – my battery is on 12 percent – I need to charge my phone – could you let William know?"

"I'm pretty sure he'll have it figured out when I go to the house with Billy instead of you..."

"Thanks – bye!"

"Give me your phone..." Dante commanded. I gave him my phone, he turned it off, and plugged it in... "Get up..." I stood up in front of him. He picked me up in his arms and carried me into the bedroom... "Now..." he said as he placed me on the bed... "I'm going to make love to you – and I'm not going to stop..." he said as he started to get undressed. I watched him intently as he took off his clothes. When he dropped his pants, his dick sprang to attention... "You want this?" he asked as he shook his dick...

"Yeess..."

"Say it..."

"I want you Dante..."

"Again..." he commanded as he climbed up on the bed and spread my legs...

"I want you Dante..."

"I want you too..." he breathed as he bent down to kiss me. He entered me as we continued kissing...

"Mmmph...   Mmmph...   Mmmph... Mmmph..."

"Mmmm... Mmmm... Mmmm... Mmmm..."

"Mmmph...   Mmmph...   Mmmph... Mmmph..."

"Mmmm... Mmmm... Mmmm... Mmmm..."

We rolled around on the bed, kissing and loving until it started getting dark...

"Dante... I..."

"Don't make me stop... Please..."

"I need to go..."

"I need you to stay..."

"Dante... I... Shit... I'm cumming again..."

"I'm cumming with you..."

"Dante... Dante... Dante..."

"Demi... Demi... Demi..."

"I don't wanna leave..."

"It'll be over soon..."

"Not soon enough..."

"I agree..."

"I have something to tell you..."

"No... Please... I don't wanna hear it..."

"Yes... You do..."

"Okay..." he sighed as he propped himself up...

"There was one time we had sex in the office..."

"I don't wanna hear this..."

"Let me finish..."

"Okay..."

"When we were finished, he told me 'Go wash your ass'..."

"He said it like that?"

"Yes..."

"Is that what you wanted to tell me?"

"No..."

"Okay – go 'head..."

"So... I got in the shower... I closed my eyes... and..."

"What happened?"

"I pushed my fingers inside me..."

"Oohhh..."

"I was cumming..."

"Okay..." he breathed as he started playing with my clit...

"I started calling your name..."

"Say my name..." he commanded as he pushed his fingers inside me...

"Dante..."

"Again..."

"Dante..."

"Cum for me..."

"DANTEEE!!" I moaned as I squirted all over his hand...

"Is that what happened?"

"Almost..." I breathed...

"Almost?" he asked as he began fucking me with his fingers again...

"I got caught..."

"Oh shit!!" he exclaimed as he snatched his hand out... "Did he hear you?!"

"I thought so – but when he asked me what I was doing I told him I decided to take a shower..."

"What'd he say?"

"He told me to hurry up and come upstairs..."

"So..." he breathed as he kissed me... "I didn't get a chance to make you cum..." he breathed as he pushed his fingers inside me and began fucking me with his fingers again...

"Huh... No..."

"Let me fix that right now..." he growled as he took my breast in his mouth and sucked my nipple hard while increasing the intensity of his fingers...

"Dante... Dante... Dante..."

"I love the way you moan my name when you cum..."

"Dante... Dante... Yes... Yes... DANTEEE!!" He continued to fuck me with his fingers as I squirmed to get away...

"Uh uh – I've waited too long for this..." he breathed as he pushed his tongue in my mouth and continued...

"Mmm... Mmm... Mmm... Mmm..." He was enjoying this more than I was as I continued to squirm...

"Hear that pussy talkin' to me?! That's mine – You hear me?! Mine!!"

"Yes Dante... Yes..."

"Say it!!"

"It's yours Dante... IT'S YYOOUURRSSS!!" He slowed down a bit but he didn't stop. He took his fingers out, waived them at me, and then he licked them...

"Mmm..." he moaned as he licked his fingers. I started to get up but he pushed me back down on the bed...

"Dante... I..."

"Shut up..." he growled as he dove between my legs...

"Dante... it's... sensitive..."

"So what..." he breathed as he went back to licking and sucking. I tried to get up again but he wasn't having it... "You try that again and I'll cuff you to the bed..."

"Dante... I..." I continued to squirm as he swirled his tongue around my clit and then he stuck in tongue inside me... "Dante... Dante... Dante... DANTEEE!!!"

"Mmmm..." he moaned as he licked, sucked, and slurped until he was satisfied... "Whose pussy is this?"

"Yours..."

"Damn right is is..." he breathed as he got up...

"Can I ask you something?"

"Sure..."

"Do you ever fantasize about me when...? Never mind..."

"I always fantasize about you..."

"Really?"

"Yes..."

"Every time?"

"You can go now..."

"Excuse me?"

"You can go now..."

"Okay..." I sighed as I got up and got dressed... "I'll see you soon..." I said as I went to leave...

"Where the fuck do you think you're going?"

"Home..."

"Get your ass over here..." he breathed as he pulled me into a kiss and kissed me hard... "I love you..."

"I love you too..."

"*M*ommy!" Billy greeted as he ran towards me...

"Hey Billy..." I sighed as we hugged each other...

"Where the fuck were you?!" William gritted...

"I'm sorry – I got stuck in traffic..." I answered as I sat down...

"That's funny..." he said as he came and sat down beside me... "I've been watching News 12... and there wasn't any fuckin' traffic! Where the fuck were you?!"

"Stop yelling at Mommy!" Billy cried...

"Come here Billy..." Dawn commanded...

"No! I want Mommy!" he cried as he ran over towards me...

"Calm down Billy – Daddy's yelling at me because he tried to call me and I didn't answer the phone so he thought something happened..."

"Are you okay Mommy?" he sniffed...

"Yes Baby – Mommy's phone died so I had to charge it – I forgot to turn it back on after I charged it – I'm sorry Honey – I should've called you and let you know I was okay..."

"Still doesn't explain where you were..." Dawn mumbled...

"I guess I'll go make dinner..." I sighed as I got up...

"Dawn already made dinner..."

"Thank you Dawn..." I said...

"Somebody had to make sure my son ate..."

"I'm sure his father would've made sure he ate – but thank you for cooking dinner – I appreciate it..."

"I did it for my son..."

"I'm sure you cooked for William too..."

"Yes she did – and it wasn't lasagna..." he added sarcastically...

"I hope you ate wherever you were – I only cooked enough for the three of us..." she said as she smiled a sinister smile...

"Yea – I had a few granola bars – since I was stuck in traffic – but if I had gone somewhere to eat, I would've brought back food..."

"I'm sorry you didn't eat Mommy..." Billy sighed...

"I'll be fine Billy – I can order some pizza on Uber Eats...

"Can I have some pizza?"

"No you can't – what you can do is go get ready for bed..." Dawn said...

"But Mommy lets me stay up until 9..." he wined...

"When was this decided?"

"We decided a couple of weeks ago..." I answered...

"We? Who's we?"

"Me and William – right Honey?"

"You decided – I never agreed to it..."

"So I have to go to bed?"

"No Billy – you can stay up until 9 – you've been doing well in school and you don't give us any trouble getting up for school..."

"Thank you Mommy..."

"You're welcome – go get ready to take a bath and then you can say good night to your mother..." I said as I took out my phone and turned it on... "Oh my God – 15 missed calls – Honey – I'm sorry..."

"You will be..." he mumbled...

"What?"

"Nothing..."

"What are you doing?" Dawn asked...

"Umm... using my phone?"

"I hope you're not ordering pizza..." I ignored her ass and ordered...

"Demi?"

"Yes Honey?"

"Why didn't you have your location on?"

"What are you talking about?"

"I tracked your phone up until you got near Stamford Mall – your location was turned off after that..."

"My phone died. When I called Dawn my phone was at 12 percent. I turned my phone off so I could charge it. When the battery dies or the phone is turned off, the location is disabled because it relies on power to function..." Dawn looked at him and he looked back at her as I went to get the door...

"Is that your pizza Mommy?"

"Yes Baby..."

"Can I have some pizza? Please?"

"It's too late for you to be eating so close to your bedtime – but I can save you some so you can have it tomorrow when you get home from school – okay?"

"Okay Mommy – Good night Mommy..."

"Good night Billy..." Dawn replied...

"Dawn – Dante won't be upset that you're coming home so late or that you already had dinner?" I asked deliberately...

"Dante is none of your fucking business!"

"You're right – Billy go get in the tub – it's getting close to 9 – good night Dawn..." I said as I got up and took the pizza into the kitchen...

"Good night – I'll see you tomorrow William..."

"See you tomorrow..." he said as she left. He waited for Billy to close the bathroom door before he came into the kitchen... "I'm gonna ask you one more time – where the fuck were you?"

"Oh my God will you stop it already!"

"You don't wanna tell me where the fuck you were?! Fine!" he exclaimed as he picked up the box of pizza, threw it on the floor, and stepped on it..."

"Wow – you are so fuckin' immature..." I said as I tried to walk past him...

"Get your ass back in here!" he gritted as he grabbed me, threw me into the stove, and I hurt my back on one of the knobs...

"OUCH!"

"You think that hurt – that's nothing compared to what I'm about to do..."

"LEAVE MOMMY ALONE!" Billy screamed as he pushed his father down. Now I was scared...

"I'm going to beat the shit outta you..." he gritted...

"No you're not – Billy – go to your room – and lock the door – GO NOW!" Billy ran in his room and locked the door...

"I'm gonna break that door down..." he said as he got up... "I'm gonna beat his ass... and then I'm gonna beat yours..."

"No – c'mon – let's go upstairs – I'll tell you where I was..."

"So you did go somewhere?"

"Yes..."

"Where'd you go?"

"I'll tell you when we go upstairs..."

"You'll tell me now..."

"C'mon – I wanna go upstairs..."

"Why can't you tell me right now?"

"You're angry..."

"I have every right to be..."

"C'mon..." I said as I took his hand... "Let's go upstairs...I'll make it up to you..."

"Okay... We'll go upstairs..." he agreed...

"Oh thank God..." I mumbled...

"What did you say?"

"Nothing – c'mon..." I said as I pulled him towards the stairs...

"Okay – we're upstairs – now where the fuck were you?!"

"I went out to happy hour..."

"Where?"

"In Stamford..."

"Why the fuck didn't you just tell me that?"

"I didn't tell you that because I didn't want Dawn to know where I was..."

"So this is about Dawn?"

"Yes..."

"You're lying..."

"I'm telling you the truth..."

"Were you really stuck in traffic?"

"Yes..."

"So when did you decide to go to happy hour?"

"I was stuck in traffic. I called Dawn. My phone died. I got off at exit 6, I went to happy hour, I left at 7, and I came home..."

"How long were you there?"

"I got there a little after 6..."

"Hmm... Okay..."

"You don't believe me?"

"I don't wanna talk anymore..." he breathed as he pulled me into a kiss..."

"What do you want to do?"

"You know what I want..." I took off my clothes and went to get in the shower... "Where are you going?"

"I'm going to get in the shower..."

"I'll join you..." I smiled to myself and went into the bathroom. He came up behind me before I could turn on the water, turned me around, and pulled me into his arms... "Don't EVER lie to me again..." he breathed as he kissed me hard...

"I won't... I promise..."

"Get your ass in the shower and spread your legs..." I did as I was told. He got in the shower, turned on the water, and laughed manically when I jumped because it was ice cold. I shivered under the water until the temperature was comfortable. He stepped into the shower, stepped towards me, picked my chin up, and looked in my eyes. He was looking for fear but I returned his gaze with lust... "You want me..."

"Yeesss..." I wasn't lying. I wanted him to fuck me because I knew my pussy would make him forget how angry he was at Billy...

"Hey..." Dawn greeted...

"Hey..."

"I'm sorry I'm so late..."

"It's okay..."

"No it's not – Demi claimed she was stuck in traffic a little after 6 – here it is damn near 9 – I had to cook something or Billy wouldn't've had anything to eat!"

"Really? His father couldn't cook him something to eat?"

"He could've – but since I was there I offered to cook..."

"Hmmm – that was nice – did you bring me anything?"

"Oh no – you didn't eat? I'm sorry – I figured you would've had something..."

"So what time did Demi get home?"

"She got home a little after 8..."

"Why are you just getting here now?"

"I'm sorry – they – no she – changed Billy's bedtime to 9 so I stayed longer to say good night to him..."

"Did you tuck him in too?" Dante asked sarcastically...

"No I didn't tuck him in – I'm sorry I wasn't here sooner..."

"Did you eat dinner?"

"Yes..."

"So... You had dinner... with them..."

"Yea..."

"I guess I'll go in the kitchen and make myself a sandwich..." he sighed as he went to go in the kitchen. Dawn went into the bedroom and started getting ready for bed...

"I ate too..." Dante mumbled under his breath. He smiled to himself as he thought about what happened earlier. He sat down at the kitchen table and gazed out the window as he ate the sandwich he made...

"Damn – I should've brought him home something to eat..." she said as she got undressed... "I was so busy cooking for them I didn't even think to stop and pick up something for him – I need to do better before I lose him..." she sighed as she slipped into her blue lingerie...

"Hey..." Dante sighed as he walked into their bedroom...
"Hey..."
"You look nice..."
"You like it?"
"I like it very much... that color suits you..." he answered as we walked towards her and pulled her into his arms...
"Dante..." she started to say...
"Shhh..." he whispered as he kissed her. Before she could say anything else, he picked her up in his arms and took her to bed.

"*G*ood morning..." he whispered as he kissed me gently and moved my hair away from my face...

"Good morning..."

"It's time to get Billy up for school..."

"Okay..." I jumped up and started my routine. I went to take a shower and when he didn't join me I was worried... "Why didn't you join me?"

"I've been up for a while..."

"Oh..." I got dressed without speaking and made sure I kept my head down because if he looked in my eyes, he'd see that I was afraid...

"I'm going to talk to Billy before he leaves for school..."

"I'll come with you..."

"I don't need you to come with me..."

"I mean — I have to go downstairs anyway — we can go together — I can make myself a cup of coffee while you talk to him..."

"Okay — c'mon..." I let him lead the way because I started shaking...

"Good morning Mommy, good morning Daddy..."

"Good morning Billy — we need to talk..." he said as he took Billy by his arm, walked him back into his room, and closed the door. I went into the kitchen to make coffee. My hands trembled as I put the water in the kettle, I spilled coffee on the counter, and I dropped the creamer on the floor. Thank God the cap was still on...

"Yes Daddy?" Billy asked tearfully...

"Why did you push me last night?"

"Because you hurt Mommy..." he answered as he started crying...

"Stop that damn crying!" Billy sniffed, wiped his face, and stood there... "I didn't hurt your mother — she's fine — you saw her just now — right?!"

"Yyeessss..."

"I didn't hurt your mother last light — I pulled her back into the kitchen because we weren't done talking — it was an accident..."

"So you didn't mean to hurt Mommy?"

"I didn't mean to hurt your mother — but you meant to hurt me — and that's a problem..."

"I'm sorry Daddy..."

"No you're not..."

"But Daddy!"

"You knew what you were doing when you pushed me down – and now you have to suffer the consequences..." he said as he went towards Billy...

"No Daddy... Please... I'm sorry... DADDY! NOOOO!" William picked up the PS5 PlayStation, held it above his head, and smashed it to pieces in front of him...

"DADDY!" he cried...

"STOP THAT FUCKIN' CRYING OR I'LL GIVE YOU SOMETHING TO CRY FOR!" he gritted as he inched closer. Billy stopped crying, wiped his face, and stood there. I waited in the living room and was sipping my coffee when he came out Billy's room... "I'm going upstairs to get dressed – I'll see you later..."

"Umm – I don't get a kiss?"

"I said I'll see you later..." he repeated as he continued upstairs. I gulped down my coffee and hurried into his room...

"He... broke... my... game..." Billy cried...

"Shhh – stop crying – he'll come back..."

"I hate him..."

"C'mon – let's go – we can talk in the car..." I said as I took his hand and pulled him out the room. I opened the front door, pulled him outside, and unlocked the doors... "Get in the car..." Billy did as he was told. I got in, we both put on our seat belts, and I started the car. I drove for two blocks and then I stopped the car...

"Why are we stopping Mommy?"

"You can cry now..."

"I don't understand..."

"You can cry now Billy..." He sat there for a few moments and I watched the tears stream down his face. I took his hand and held it as he continued crying...

"I hate him..." he mumbled...

"Say it again..."

"You want me to say it again Mommy?"

"Yes Billy..."

"I hate him!"

"Say it louder..."

"I HATE HIM!"

"AGAIN!"

"I HATE HIM! I MEANT TO PUSH HIM AND I'M NOT SORRY! UUGGHHH!" We sat there for a few moments and I watched his chest heaving. His face was beat red. He'd been holding back his feelings because he was afraid and now that he was releasing them, I could see traits of his father...

"How do you feel?"

"Huh?"

"How do you feel?"

"I feel better Mommy..."

"That's good..." I said as I started the car...

"I love you Mommy...

"I love you too – put your seat belt back on...

"Mommy?"

"Yes Billy?"

"Daddy said it was an accident – is that true?"

"Yes Billy..."

"Okay..." It was an accident alright – an accident that wouldn't've happened in the first place if he hadn't thrown me into the stove – but whatever... "Mommy?"

"Yes Billy?"

"Can we get pizza after school?"

"You know what – that's a great idea – we'll go for pizza after school..."

"Okay – have a good day Mommy..."

"You too..."

"Get in here..." William said as he pulled Dawn inside..."

"Did you ever find out where she was last night?"

"Did you come here to talk or did you come here to fuck?!"

"I came here to fuck..." she sighed...

"Are you sure?"

"Yes – I'm sure..."

"Get your ass upstairs then..."

"I don't know how you can still fuck her after you fuck me like that..."

"I'm a man – I like pussy..."

"So that's it? I'm just pussy to you?"

"Basically..."

"Damn – that's fucked up..."

"We're divorced – right?"

"I know... but..."

"But what?"

"I thought we were something more..."

"You're Billy's mother – you'll always be a part of my life – but if you wanted more we'd still be married..."

"I did want more – you're the one that changed..."

"You know what – I'm not having this conversation with you – and if this is what you're gonna do when you come over here – don't come back – I like pussy – I don't like headaches..."

"Okay – I'm sorry I brought it up – I'll stop..."

"Good..."

"Can I as you something though?"

"What?"

"Do you love her?"

"Yea – I love her..." Dawn's heart sank. William knew he hurt her but he didn't give a fuck – why should he? "Let me ask you this – do you love him?"

"I care about him..."

"Do you love him?"

"No..."

"Does he know that?"

"No..."

"Why are you with him then?"

"Because he loves me..."

"Hmmm..." Dawn didn't say anything else. She went to the bathroom and Billy's door was open...

"Oh my God! What happened in here?!"

"In where?"

"In Billy's room?!"

"I broke his game..."

"I paid $600 for that fuckin' game! Why the fuck did you break it?!" William got up off the couch, walked over to her and got up in her face...

"I broke it because that lil' mutha fucka pushed me down in the kitchen...

"WHAT?! THAT'S NOT LIKE HIM!! WHY?!"

"Because he saw me throw Demi into the stove..."

"WHAT THE HELL IS WRONG WITH YOU?!"

"Who the fuck do you think you're talking to?!" he gritted as he grabbed her throat...

"I'm... I'm sorry... I..."

"That's more like it..." he breathed as he kissed her...

"What happened?"

"I asked her where the fuck she was and she wouldn't tell me so I picked up the box of pizza, threw it on the floor, and stomped on it..."

"Damn – you were really pissed..."

"I wasn't pissed off until she told me I was being immature..."

"WHAT?!"

"Yea..."

"Is that when you threw her into the stove?"

"I didn't really throw her into the stove – I grabbed her and threw her back into the kitchen

– she just happened to hit the stove on her way back in..." he laughed...

"And Billy saw this?"

"Yea..."

"That's not good..."

"If he had stayed in his fuckin' room and minded his business – he'd still have his game..."

"That doesn't make you right..."

"It's time for you to go..." he said as he took her by the arm...

"Let go of me..."

"I'm about to..." he said as he opened the front door, pushed her out, and slammed the door in her face.

"Good morning..." Dante answered...

"It's me..."

"Hey you..."

"Can you come meet me for lunch?"

"You want us to be seen in public?"

"No – I want you to meet me at the Marriott in Stamford..."

"I'd love to meet you at the Marriott – I just don't think it's a good idea..."

"The Business Council of Westchester is having their Annual Lunch at the Marriott – my company is one of the sponsors so I bought 100 tickets. I also got three rooms..."

"On the company card?"

"Yea..."

"Are we signed up for the event?"

"I'm signed up under my company..."

"So no one will question why you're there..."

"Nope..."

"We can't really be seen together..."

"I'm not really feeling that well – I think I'll go to one of the rooms and lay down..."

"What room will you be in?"

"315..."

"I'll see you soon..."

"Who is it?"

"Room Service..." I ran to the door and flung it open. We were all over each other as soon as he pushed the door closed...

"Mmmm... Mmm... Mmm... Mmm..."

"Mmmph... Mmmph... Mmmph... Mmmph..."

"Mmmm... Mmm... Mmm... Mmm..."

"Mmmph... Mmmph... Mmmph... Mmmph..."

I wrapped my arms around his neck and my legs around his waist. Dante carried me to bed, fell down on top of me, and we picked up where we left off...

"Mmmm... Mmm... Mmm... Mmm..."

"Mmmph... Mmmph... Mmmph... Mmmph..."

"Mmmm... Mmm... Mmm... Mmm..."

"Mmmph... Mmmph... Mmmph... Mmmph..."

"You wanna talk about it?" Dante knew me so well...

"I'm ready to leave him..."

"Are you serious?!"

"Yes Dante..."

"What happened?"

"It was bad..."

"Come here..." he breathed as he pulled me close to him and held me. I burst into tears and cried for a few moments. He didn't speak – he waited for me to stop crying and when I did, he kissed me... "You know I love you – right?"

"Yes Dante..."

"Good. Get up and get dressed. I'm going to order room service and we can talk while we eat..."

"I wish I could stay in bed with you..."

"You'll be able to stay in bed with me soon..."

"Promise?"

"Hell yea..." he breathed as he got up. He called to order room service after we got dressed...

"Who is it?" I asked...

"Room Service..." I motioned for Dante to hide and then I went to answer the door...

"Thank you..."

"You're welcome – have a nice day..."

"What did you get us?"

"I got us burgers and fries..."

"That'll work..." I said as I pushed the cart over by the table and sat down. Dante came to sit down and he took the cover off the food...

"These look good..."

"They do look good..." I said as I picked up the burger and took a bite...

"What happened last night?"

"He kept asking me where the fuck were you – Billy started crying and ran to me after he told his father to stop yelling at me..."

"And this bitch wants to keep fuckin' him..."

"Exactly! So I stuck to my story..."

"I'm sorry Demi – I don't know how you were able to sit and eat with them..."

"I didn't – she told me she hoped I got something to eat because she only cooked enough for them..."

"WHAT?!"

"I thanked her for cooking for them anyway..."

"That fuckin' bitch – she cooked for that mutha fucka and made sure you didn't eat – and she didn't stop to pick up anything for me to eat either..."

"You didn't eat last night?"

"I had a sandwich..."

"I didn't eat at all..."

"You weren't hungry?"

"I ordered pizza – Billy wanted some but Dawn said he couldn't have any so I told him I would save him some and he could eat it today after school..."

"So you did eat..."

"No..."

"Why not?"

"William came into the kitchen and asked me where the fuck I was again..."

"Oh no..."

"I stuck to my story so he threw the pizza on the floor and stomped on it..."

"I can't believe Dawn still wants to fuck that mutha fucka..."

"So I told him he was immature... I tried to leave the kitchen... and..."

"Oh no..."

"He grabbed me... he threw me into the stove... I hurt my back... and..."

"Tell me!" Dante gritted...

"Billy saw him..."

"No..." Dante whispered...

"Billy pushed William on the floor and screamed at him to leave me alone..." I said as I started crying...

"Did he... did he hurt Billy?"

"I told Billy to go in his room and lock the door..."

"Did he hurt Billy?!"

"He said he was going to break the door down... beat his ass... and then he was going to beat mine..."

"OH MY GOD! WHAT DID HE DO TO BILLY?! WHAT DID HE DO TO YOU?!"

"I convinced him to go upstairs – I told him I'd tell him where I was..."

"You wanted to protect Billy..."

"Yes..."

"What did you tell him?"

"I told him I went to happy hour..."

"Did he believe you?"

"I don't think so... he kept asking questions – but my location showed Stamford so I wasn't worried..."

"Did you sleep with him?"

"Yes..."

"Shit!"

"Aren't you still sleeping with Dawn?"

"That's different..."

"How?"

"I'm a man – I have needs..."

"Did you have needs last night?"

"I didn't have a need – I had an opportunity..."

"I loved him in the beginning..."

"I still love her – even though I know she's fuckin' him..."

"You just told me you love me..."

"I do love you..."

"I love you too..."

"You love me?"

"Yes Dante..."

"You said he hurt your back..."

"Yes..."

"Let me see..." I stood up and turned towards him so he could look at my back... "You're bruised..."

"I know..."

"Does it hurt?"

"Yes..." Dante started kissing my back and I stopped him...

"Dante... Stop..."

"Why?"

"Because... If you don't stop... I'll get back in bed with you..."

"So..."

"So I need to tell you what happened this morning..."

"Oh my God... Did he hurt Billy?"

"He got up early this morning. He said he needed to talk to him. I was scared..."

"I'm scared and you haven't even told me what happened yet..."

"He went into the room with Billy while I made coffee. I didn't hear anything at first – but then I heard Billy scream..."

"Oh my God... Please tell me Billy's okay?"

"William picked up his PS5 and smashed it to pieces..."

"Aww..."

"I heard William tell him to stop fuckin' crying so I hurried into the room and hushed him so William wouldn't come back downstairs..."

"That poor kid..."

"I drove around the corner, turned off the car, and told him he could cry..."

"Did he?"

"Yes... and then he started to mumble that he hated his father..."

"Oh shit!"

"I told him to say it again..."

"Why?"

"Because that's how he feels..."

"Thank God his father doesn't know about that..."

"I saw traits of his father..."

"You did?"

"Yes - I told him to say it again and he started yelling he hated his father and he wasn't sorry he pushed him..."

"Oh shit!"

"He's going to be just like his father when he grows up..."

"Don't say that..."

"I asked him how he felt after he calmed down and he told me he felt good..."

"Oohhh..."

"And I told him that was good..."

"Why would you tell him that?"

"Because it was good that he let that out – if he didn't – he would've had a bad day – he might've even flipped out on the teacher..."

"You really love Billy..."

"Yes..."

"He's going to be devastated when you leave..."

"It's going to break my heart..."

"At least he has his mother..."

"A lot of good she'll do..."

"Maybe they'll get back together..."

'I'm taking him out for pizza after school..."

"Are you sure you're ready to leave Demi?"

"Yes Dante..."

"I just want you to be sure because once we put things in motion - there's no turning back..."

"I know..."

"So how we doin' this?"

"I'm filing for divorce..."

"Are you serious?!"

"Yes Dante... I have to..."

"I agree – but he'll never agree to a divorce..."

"He won't know what hit him..."

"What... How..."

"I'll prepare the taxes. I'll put a bunch of papers in front of him, I'll go through the pages, and I'll tell him sign here, sign, here, sign here..."

"He'll fall for that?"

"I'll give him some pussy first..."

"Dammit! Did you have to say that?!"

"I'm sorry Dante..."

"Did he make you sign a pre-nup?"

"Yes..."

"How are you going to get him to give you a divorce with a pre-nup in place?"

"I'm asking for an uncontested divorce – besides – I don't want anything from him anyway..."

"So he signs the papers – what happens when he gets served?"

"He's not going to get served – you are..."

"Ooohhh..."

"You'll sign for the papers – I'll file them – the divorce decree will be mailed to you – we'll apply for a marriage license – we'll wait 48 hours – and then we'll go to Vegas and get married..."

"Did you just ask me to marry you?"

"Yes Dante...If you'll marry me · will you marry me?" He jumped up from the table, pulled me into his arms, and kissed me hard...

"Yes – I'll marry you Demi!"

"There's one more thing..."

"What?"

"We can't move in together right away..."

"WHAT?! WHY?!"

"After we come back from Vegas you need to go back to Dawn and I need to go back to William..."

"SO – YOU EXPECT ME TO LET YOU GO BACK TO WILLIAM AFTER WE GET MARRIED?!"

"Here me out – if you don't like it – we won't do it..."

"Okay..."

"So – I go back to William – you go back to Dawn. I send you a message to come get me. When you get there – we drop a bomb on both of them. We tell them we know they've been fuckin' and so have we – and then we tell them they can have each other because we're married. When William tries to say I can't be married to you because I'm married to him – you present him with our divorce decree..."

"Damn Demi – you're really ready to leave!"

"That man has choked me. He pushed my face in a plate of food and tried to force me to eat it in front of Dawn and Billy. He threw me into the stove last night in front of Billy and promised to beat his ass and mine. I've come home from work to that bitch being in my bedroom, helping herself to whatever's in the fridge as if she put food in there, saying whatever the fuck she wants because he doesn't make it clear to her that she needs to respect boundaries, dropping by unannounced, and then they're both trying to bullshit me with the co-parenting cumbaya – and he's still fuckin' her – damn right I'm ready to leave both their asses – I'm just sorry that Billy's going to end up like his father..."

"Me too..."

"So you'll do it?"

"I'll do it – under one condition..."

"Name it..."

"Once we get married – that's my pussy – and it's locked..."

"I need to go get Billy – I promised him we'd go for pizza..."

"Did you hear me?" he said as he pulled me into his arms...

"Yes Dante..." I breathed as I kissed him... "I heard you..."

"*H* i Mommy!"

"Hey Billy – how was your day?"

"I had fun today Mommy!"

"Mrs. Taylor?"

"Yes?"

"I'm Ms. Anderson – Billy's teacher – can we talk?"

"Am I in trouble?" Billy asked...

"No Billy..."

"Okay – I'll wait in the classroom..." he said as he skipped down the hall...

"Mrs. Taylor – Billy came into class very hyper today..."

"Ohh... Because I told him we were going for pizza?"

"Yes – and some of the other kids felt bad..."

"Oh no – I'm sorry..."

"I'd like to do something for the class... and... I was thinking..."

"Yes?"

"Well... I'd like to get pizza for the class for lunch tomorrow..."

"That's nice..."

"Well... I don't know how to say this..."

"Just tell me..." I sighed...

"Some of the other parents can't contribute..."

"How many pies do you need?"

"Ten pies should do it – I'll contribute..."

"I'll have 10 pies delivered to you tomorrow at 11:45..."

"Oh my God – thank you so much!"

"You're welcome..."

"Mommy – can we go now?"

"Yes Billy – Nice meeting you Ms. Anderson..."

"Nice meeting you too – thanks again..."

"Billy – I need you to go sit down at the table – I'm going to place the order – okay?"

"Okay Mommy!" he exclaimed as he skipped over to the table and sat down...

"Good evening – can I take your order?"

"I'd like 10 pizzas delivered to Ms. Anderson at Orange Avenue Elementary School in Milford..."

"We don't deliver outside of Stamford..."

"Good evening – I'm Nick – I'm the manager here – how can I help you?"

"I need 10 pizzas delivered to Ms. Anderson at Orange Avenue Elementary School in Milford..."

"When do you need them?"

"I need them delivered tomorrow morning at 11:45 a.m...."

"We don't deliver outside of Stamford but I can call Milford Pizza and put the order in for you..."

"Thank you..."

"You're welcome – will you be dinning here tonight?"

"Yes – Billy – what kind of pizza do you want?"

"Can I get pepperoni?"

"Sure – Can I have a small pepperoni to stay and two large pepperonis to go?"

"Got it – will that be cash or charge?"

"Charge..." I answered as I handed him my card...

"Should I use this card for your order at Milford too?"

"Yes please..."

"Okay – you got it..."

"Mommy – can I have some soda?"

"Yes Billy – but you can't drink it until after you eat..." I answered as I took a ginger ale and a Hawaiian Fruit Punch out the cooler, took it to the table, and sat down...

"Thank you Mommy..."

"You're welcome..." I sat there and watched Billy smiling as he played with the menu on the table. I felt bad because I knew I'd have to break his heart...

"Here you go..." the server said...

"Thank you!" Billy exclaimed...

"Billy – wait – that's hot..."

"Okay..." he sighed...

"Billy – I need you to do something for me..."

"Yes Mommy?"

"I need you to keep what happened this morning a secret..."

"I can't tell Mommy?"

"No..."

"But I promised Mommy I would never keep a secret from her..."

"I know – but if you tell her – she'll tell your father – and he'll be mad..."

"Okay – I won't tell her..."

"Good..." I said as I put a piece of pizza on the plate for him...

"Mommy?"

'Yes Baby..."

"Are you going to tell on me?"

"For what?"

"For saying I hate Daddy..."

"No..."

"I don't hate Daddy... But I think Daddy hates me..."

"Oh no Baby – Daddy loves you very much..."

"He does?"

"Yes..."

"Why is he mean to me then?"

"He doesn't mean it – he just wants you to be strong so nobody picks on you..."

"Why is he mean to you then? You're not mean to him..."

"I don't think he's mean to me on purpose – I think he doesn't know better..."

"But he's an adult!"

"I know..." I sighed... "Billy?"

"Yes Mommy?"

"Did your father hit your mother?" He stopped eating his pizza and put his head down... "It's okay Billy..." I said as I touched his hand... We don't have to talk about it..."

"He hit Mommy..."

"I'm sorry..."

"He was mean to Mommy too..."

"Aww..."

"He doesn't love Mommy anymore..."

"He still likes your mother and they both love you..."

"Are you going to leave Daddy if he keeps being meant to you?"

"Oh shoot – we need to hurry up – your mother has to help you with your homework – let's finish this pizza so we can go home..."

"Excuse me miss – your pizzas are ready to go..."

"Thank you..." I said as I took my last bite, got up from the table, got the pizza, and headed home...

"Hi Mommy! Hi Daddy!"

"Hey Billy – where were you?" Dawn asked...

"Mommy took me out for pizza!"

"That's nice – it would've been nice if you called..."

"Hi Dawn – I brought you a box of pizza to take home to Dante so you don't have to stop and pick up dinner for him..."

"I told you before – Dante is none of your business..."

"That was considerate..." William said...

"Thank you – could you take these boxes in the kitchen? I bought us a large pepperoni – I figured we could eat while Dawn helps Billy with his homework..."

"Sure..." he answered as he smiled. Dawn was seething as he took the boxes from me and we went into the kitchen... "Come sit with me..." I sat down at the table... "I over-reacted last night... I'm sorry..." I burst into tears... "Please... don't cry... I'm sorry..." I stopped crying, wiped my eyes, and opened the box of pizza...

"You want me to get plates?"

"No – we can eat out the box..." He kept smiling at me as we ate. I smiled back at him but I didn't trust him...

"Billy's done with his homework so I'm gonna head out..." Dawn interrupted...

"Don't forget the pizza..." I said. Dawn snatched the box and turned to leave...

"Bye Mommy!" Billy exclaimed as he hurried out his room to give her a hug...

"Bye Billy – I'll see you tomorrow..."

"Mommy – can I watch tv for a little while?"

"Sure..."

"Okay!" he exclaimed as he hurried back into his room...

"You want a Heineken?"

"Yea..." William took four bottles out the fridge...

"Why so many?"

"The other bottles are coming upstairs with us..." he answered as he smiled at me mischievously...

"Hey Babe – I got you some pizza..." Dawn lied...

"Oh wow – you went to planet Pizza in Stamford? Is that why you're late?"

"Yes..." she lied. Dante laughed to himself...

"Thank you Demi..." he whispered as Dawn left him in the kitchen.

"*D*emi..."

"Yes?"

"What are you working on?"

"Taxes..."

"We have an accountant for that..." he laughed...

"I know – but he always complains when he has to do the Schedule C so I put everything in QuickBooks..."

"Oh... Okay..."

"After I print it out, I'll need you to sign a few papers..."

"Why am I signing papers now before we go file?"

"I'm still paying on my student loans- they always ask me for my spouse information..."

"When are you going to be done with those payments anyway?"

"Well – since I work for the County – I get complete forgiveness after I've made payments for 10 years..."

"How many years have you paid so far?"

"Seven..."

"Didn't you qualify for student loan forgiveness under Biden's plan?"

"I applied for it – but I haven't heard anything yet – besides – I get to claim the interest paid on the taxes..."

"You get to claim student loan interest on your taxes?!"

"Yup..."

"I didn't know that..."

"Oh yea – they sent me a statement..." I said as I showed him the statement...

"Hmmm – that's good – but why do I have to sign?"

"Because we're married..."

"I still don't understand it..."

"Basically I'm just telling them I'm not single anymore..."

"Won't they raise your payments if my income is added?"

"They might..."

"What are you going to do if that happens?"

"I'll apply for forbearance until I get forgiveness..." I laughed...

"Okay..." I waited for him to leave before I took out my phone and googled information for an uncontested divorce in Connecticut. As soon as I started looking at the requirements, I realized it wasn't going to be easy... "Shit!"

"What's wrong?" William asked as he came into the office...

"Oh – nothing – I put in for a personal day at work and they're not approving it..."

"You almost done?"

"Yea..."

"Hurry up..."

"Okay..." I waited for him to leave and then I sent Dante a text message...

"I can't do it..."

"Why?!"

"Click on the link I sent you – it's not as simple as I thought – it's going to cost me a minimum of $5k – and how am I going to get all those documents together without him finding out?"

"Don't freak out. Take a break and go back to it tomorrow..."

"Okay..."

"I love you..."

"I love you too..."

"You comin'?" he asked as he came back inside...

"Yea..." I turned off the computer, I got up, and William smiled at me as I walked towards him. He took my hand and led me into the bedroom. He didn't need to tell me what to do and I didn't need to tell him what I wanted. I got in bed and he got in bed beside me... "Ouch..."

"What's wrong?"

"My breasts are tender..."

"Let me make kiss them and make them feel better..." he breathed as he began to kiss them...

"That's nice..." I sighed...

"Ouch..." I said as he squeezed them...

"Hmmm... that's odd..."

"It's probably that time of the month..."

"I don't think that's it..."

"You don't?"

"Naa..."

"What do you think it is then?"

"Well..." he said and then he licked my nipples... "Usually when it's that time of the month, you're horny and wanna fuck..."

"That's true..."

"So..." he said as he kissed my breasts... "Is it possible something else is going on?"

"I don't think so..."

"Demi?"

"Yes?"

"Is there any chance you're pregnant?"

"I don't think so..."

"When was your last period?"

"Oh my God – you sound like my gynecologist!" I laughed...

"Well?"

"I haven't had my period in two months..."

"I'm going to make love to you tonight..." he breathed as he took my nipple in his mouth... "And tomorrow..." he breathed as he took the other nipple in his mouth... "You're going to buy a pregnancy test..."

"Okay..." I moaned as he kissed his way down my body...

"Hey Baby..." he breathed as he kissed around my navel... "Hey Baby..." he breathed as he got in between my legs and spread my lips... "Hey Baby..." he breathed on my clit before he began licking and sucking...

"Huh... William..."

"Mmm..." he moaned. He was driving me crazy and he knew it. I couldn't resist but I had no intention of resisting – he was right about me being horny all the time – I couldn't get enough. Thank God he has a high sex drive and an insatiable appetite for pussy because I didn't know what the hell was wrong – or right – with me...

"Damn Dante..." Dawn breathed...

"I don't know what's gotten into you..." he breathed as he kissed her... "But I like it..."

"That would be you..." she breathed as she kissed him back...

"Mmm... you're still horny..."

"Yeess..."

"I wish I could give you more..."

"Dante... don't stop..."

"I have to... I need to get ready for work..."

"Fine..." she sighed as she stopped kissing him. Dante got up out the bed, went into the bathroom, and got in the shower. Dawn joined him... "Hey..." she sighed as she came up behind him and grabbed his dick...

"Dawn... I can't..."

"C'mon Dante... you still have time..."

"I need to go..." he said as he opened the door to the shower and stepped out...

"Are you serious right now?"

"I need to get ready for work..." he answered as he toweled off. Dawn stayed in the shower as he got dressed. When she got out the shower, he was gone...

"Hey..."

"Can I see you?"

"What's wrong Dante?"

"I just need to see you..."

"I need to see you too – but we need to be careful – William has a tracker on my car..."

"Leave your car at work – take the bus – meet me at the Marriott..."

"I want to Dante but how am I going to explain being late to William?"

"I don't know – I'll help you figure it out when I see you..."

"Okay – I'll see you tonight when I get off work..."

"Hey..." Dawn sighed...

"What's wrong?"

"I need some more dick..."

"More?"

"Dante told me he had to stop because he needed to get ready for work..."

"So you just fucked him – and now you expect me to fuck you?"

"You're still fucking your wife – right?"

"I fucked her last night – I didn't fuck her this morning..."

"Are you going to fuck me or not?"

"I'm not – you can go..."

"UUUGGGHHH! I HATE YOU!"

"C'mere..." he laughed as he took her by the hand and led her upstairs...

"Oh thank God..." I sighed as I found the pregnancy tests. I shoved two into my pocket right before my nosy co-worker walked up on me...

"Good morning Demi..."

"Good morning Annette..."

"Great minds think alike..."

"Huh?"

"I like to stop here in the morning too – you try to come in here at lunch or after work – it gets crazy!"

"I know that's right!" I laughed...

"Le'me go – I need to see if my prescription is ready – I'll see you later..." she said as she hurried towards the pharmacy..."

"Did you find everything you were looking for?" the manager asked as he walked up to me...

"Yes – thank you..."

"Hmmm – okay..." he said as he walked away...

"What the fuck... Oohhh..." It dawned on me that he must've seen me put the pregnancy tests in my pocket. I rushed to the self-checkout, took them out of my pocket, and scanned them. I noticed security watching me as I put them in the paper bag. I printed the receipt and purposely held it up as I walked out...

"Have a good day..."

"Same to you..." I replied...

"Hey Demi..." Annette said as she ran up to me...

"Hey Annette – what's up?"

"Could you give me a ride back to work?"

"Sure – c'mon..." I answered as I motioned for her to follow me to the car. As soon as I sat down, I shoved the paper bag in my purse..."

"I'm glad they had your prescription – mine won't be ready until tomorrow..."

"Damn – I'm sorry..." I said as I started the car. Thank God the job was just around the corner...

"Thanks girl – I'll see you later!" she exclaimed as she jumped out the car. I got out the car and hurried inside...

"Slow down!" my manager laughed as I ran into her...

"I'm sorry..." I laughed...

"Don't worry about it..." she laughed as she went towards her office. I hurried into the bathroom and ran into the last stall at the end...

"I hope I'm not pregnant..." I sighed as I took one of the pregnancy tests out of my purse...

"Damn – I gotta pee!" I heard Annette exclaimed as she hurried into one of the stalls... "Whew! I made it!" I sat there perfectly still until I heard her flush the toilet...

"Dammit – hurry up!" I thought to myself as she washed her hands. I took advantage of the noise from the hand dryer to open the box. As soon as she left, I got up, pulled down my pants, and peed on the stick... "Now I wait..." I whispered... "Dammit!" I took my time coming out the stall. I made sure no one was in the bathroom and pushed the pregnancy test down in the garbage along with the box...

"Hey girl – you good?" Annette asked as she came back into the bathroom...

"Yea – I had business to take care of..." I laughed. Annette flew out the bathroom and I bust out laughing...

"Damn girl – you still want more?"

"Yeess..."

"Look – I need to get ready for work..."

"What is with you?"

"Me?"

"You're usually fucking the shit outta me telling me this is your pussy!"

"I made you come three times!"

"Since when did you start counting?" she laughed as she got up...

"This has been fun – but I need to get to work..."

"Alright, alright – can I wash my ass before I go?"

"Yes – downstairs..."

"Why can't I wash my ass up here?"

"Demi's like a detective – if she finds a hair in here I'll never hear the end of it..."

"Okay – I'll go downstairs. William followed behind her, she took a clean wash cloth out the linen closet, and then she went into the bathroom. William waited for her to come out.... "I'll see you tonight..."

"See you tonight..." he said as he opened the door...

"Damn – he may have a point – let me go stop by the pharmacy..." she said as she got in her car and drove off.

"*H*ey..."

"Hey Demi..."

"I'm going to be late..."

"Are you stuck in traffic again?"

"No – I'm stuck at work..."

"Overtime?"

"No – we started a new project – I work on it during the day but it's easier for me to do the statistics after everybody goes home..."

"Why do you need to wait until everybody goes home?"

"Because it's quiet..."

"Is this going to be every night?"

"No – one or two nights a week..."

"How long are you going to be?"

"I'll leave here between 6:30 and 7..."

"Can you make it 6:30?"

"I'll try..."

"Okay – I'll see you when you get home - "I love you..."

"I love you too..." It was easy to lie to him now that I knew he was still fucking Dawn... "I'm on my way Dante..." I said as I hurried out the building and ran to get the bus...

"Who is it?"

"Room service..." Dante flung the door open and pulled me inside... "Dante – wait..."

"What's wrong?"

"We need to be quick – I told William I was working late – I need to leave here by 6:30..."

"It's 5:30 now – we can make that happen..." he breathed as he pulled me into a hiss. We stripped out of our clothes on the way to the bed...

"Mmmph...   Mmmph...   Mmmph... Mmmph..."

"Mmm... Mmm... Mmm... Mmm..."

"Mmmph...   Mmmph...   Mmmph... Mmmph..."

"Mmm... Mmm... Mmm... Mmm..."

"Mmmph! Mmmph! Mmmph! Mmmph!"

"Mmm! Mmm! Mmm! Mmm!"

"Damn..." he breathed...

"I know..." I panted...

"I have a confession to make..."

"Me too..."

"I'll go first..."

"Okay..."

"I haven't been satisfying Dawn..."

"You're not fucking her anymore?"

"I'm still fucking her – but not as much as she'd like..."

"What changed?"

"You..."

"Oh so it's my fault?"

"Yes..."

"I love you..." I sighed...

"That – that's it right there..."

"What?"

"You love me..."

"I do love you... but..."

"You still love William?"

"Yea..."

"You haven't changed your mind – have you?"

"No – I still want to leave him. Ever since I found out he's still fucking Dawn – I feel like my marriage is a fraud..."

"I'm sorry..."

"I'm not..."

"Umm..."

"I was – but now that I have you..." Dante interrupted me with a kiss...

"You said you have a confession to make..."

"Yes..." I sighed...

"Oh no – what's wrong?"

"Please don't hate me..."

"I could never hate you..."

"I'm pregnant..."

"You're pregnant?"

"Yes..."

"What does that mean for us?"

"We can still be together..."

"I'm not raising that mutha fucka's child!"

"I'm not asking you to..."

"So what are you asking me?"

"I'm going to tell William I'm pregnant..."

"WHY?! HE'LL NEVER LET YOU GO!"

"We're going to go to New York..."

"William can get to New York..."

"You'll go with me to the OBGYN..."

"I just told you – I'm not raising that mutha fucka's child..."

"I'm not asking you to help me raise his child..."

"What are you asking me to do then?"

"I need you to be my husband..."

"I'm confused..."

"I'm going to go to the clinic..."

"Okay..."

"I'm going to get an abortion..."

"Ooohhh..."

"And my husband will be there to support me..."

"Me?"

"Yes..."

"Are you sure you want to have an abortion?"

"I don't want to have a baby with William..."

"What are you going to do when he wants pussy?"

"Huh?"

"You won't be able to have sex for six weeks..."

"I'll tell him I had a miscarriage..."

"What if he wants you to see the doctor?"

"I'll refuse..."

"You'll refuse?   And you think that'll work?"

"Yes..."

"Have you made the appointment yet?"

"No..."

"Won't William find out when the insurance claims come to the house?"

"I'm using someone else's insurance card..."

"I don't think that's a good idea..."

"Why not?"

"What if something goes wrong?"

"Okay – I'll use my own card – I'll just pray I get the mail before my husband does..."

"Did you ever want kids?"

"Yes..."

"I don't want kids – are you okay with that?"

"As long as you want me – that's all that matters – what time is it?"

"It's after 6..."

"I need to go..."

"Stay with me a little longer... please..."

"Soon...I said as I got up...

"Not soon enough..."

"I love you..."

"I love you too..."

"Mommy!" Billy exclaimed as I came in...

"Hey Billy – Hello Dawn..."

"Hello..."

"How was work?" William asked...

"Busy..." I answered as I went into the bathroom...

"C'mon – let's go finish your homework..." Dawn said as she took Billy by the hand and led him into the bedroom...

"Dawn – you can go in the room with Billy as soon as you get here – you don't have to wait for me to get home – especially now that I'm going to be working late a couple of nights a week..."

"That's okay – I'll wait for you – I know Billy likes to see you before he starts on his homework..."

"Billy – Mommy's going to be getting home late from work – I need you to start your homework earlier so you'll have more time to relax before you go to bed – okay?"

"Okay Mommy..." That bitch thought she was slick – she wasn't waiting for me to make sure Billy got to see me – she was waiting on me because she was clocking me – she doesn't know I caught her looking at her watch when I came in the house – plus – the sooner she helps him with is homework – the sooner she can leave...

"I agree..." William said. Dawn caught me smiling and I didn't give a fuck...

"Since it's late – how 'bout I make spaghetti with chicken, broccoli, garlic, & oil?"

"How long will that take?"

"About 20 minutes..."

"Can Mommy stay for dinner?"

"Sure..."

"Yea!" William looked at me and smiled. I went into the kitchen and started prepping while Dawn continued to help Billy with his homework...

"Dinner's ready..." William came into the kitchen and sat at the table. Billy came in with Dawn and they both sat down...

"Sit – I'll make the plates. I sat down, William got the plates out the cabinet, put the food on them, and put them on the table...

"Thank you Honey..."

"Thank you..." I couldn't wait for Dawn to finish eating. I couldn't wait for her to leave. I was ready to be done with her. I loved Billy and I knew I'd miss him – but I won't miss her ass...

"That was good..." she said...

"You're welcome..."

"It's late – I need to get home..." she said as she got up...

"Good night Mommy..."

"Good night..." William said as he walked her to the door...

"Mommy – can I watch tv?"

"Yes – but only until 9 – okay?"

"Okay Mommy..." William waited for Billy to go in his room...

"Thank you..." he breathed as he pulled me into a kiss...

"You're welcome..."

"Let's go upstairs..."

"Not yet..."

"Why?"

"I wanna wait until Billy goes to bed so we won't be disturbed..." I answered as I smiled at him mischievously...

"Hey Babe..."

"Hey – why so late?" Dante asked. We actually enjoyed pretending like we didn't know what was going on...

"Demi had to work late – and guess what?"

"What?"

"Billy asked if I could stay for dinner and Demi said yes..."

"Really?! That was nice..."

"It really was..."

"What did you have?"

"Spaghetti with chicken, broccoli, & oil..."

"Mmm – that sounds good..."

"Good – because I stopped to pick you up some..." she said as she handed him the bag...

"Billy?"

"Yes Mommy?"

"It's 9 o'clock..."

"Okay..." he sighed as he turned off the tv. We both went in his room to tell him good night...

"Good night Mommy, good night Daddy..."

"Good night..." we both said...

"I love you..."

"We love you too..." William took me by the hand and pulled me towards the stairs...

"William – wait..." He stopped and looked at me with a look of confusion. I got my purse and put it on my shoulder...

"You stopped to get your purse?"

"C'mon..." I said as I headed upstairs. He followed right behind me... "William – wait..."

"What now?!" he exclaimed. I put my purse down, opened it, and took out the pregnancy test...

"Oh my God..."

"Come with me..." I said as I motioned for him to follow me into the bathroom. I pulled down my clothes and sat down on the toilet... "Open the box." He was so excited his hands were shaking... "Hurry up – I have to pee!" He handed me the stick, I peed on it, and then I gave it to him. I got up off the toilet, pulled up my clothes, and washed my hands while he waited...

"We're having a baby..." he whispered as he started to cry...

"We're having a baby?" I asked, pretending to be surprised...

"We're having a baby!" he exclaimed as he picked me up and spun me around... "I love you so much!"

"I love you too..." He picked me up in his arms and took me to bed. He was so attentive and loving I almost felt bad but then I thought about Dawn and I realized I had him right where I wanted him.

"*G*ood morning..." he whispered in my ear..."

"Good morning..." I yawned...

"Good morning..." he breathed as he got up, turned me over, and kissed my belly button...

"That tickles..."

"I can't wait to tell Billy he's going to have a little brother or a little sister..."

"William – No..."

"Why not? Aren't you happy?"

"Can we wait a little while? Please?"

"Why?"

"Please don't be mad..."

"What's wrong?" he asked as he sat up...

"I don't want you to tell Billy because..."

"He'll tell Dawn..." he interrupted...

"Yea..."

"How long do you think we're going to be able to keep this from him?"

"I just want to wait a while – I want this to be just between us for a while – okay?"

"Okay – but once you start showing..."

"We'll tell him before I start showing..." I laughed....

"Okay..." he laughed...

"I was wondering why I was horny all the time..."

"I had a feeling you were pregnant..."

"I know you did..."

"C'mon – I need to get Billy up for school – we can talk about this later..." I said as I got up and went into the bathroom. William followed me. He waited for me to finish and continued to watch me as I washed my hands... "I'm going to make an appointment to go to the OBGYN in Manhattan..."

"Why?"

"My gynecologist doesn't deliver babies anymore..."

"Since when?"

"Since the malpractice insurance premium isn't affordable anymore..." I laughed...

"She actually told you that?'

"Yea..." I laughed...

"Why do you want to go to Manhattan? Can't you find a doctor in Stamford?"

"I could... but..."

"This is about Dawn..."

"Yes..."

"I understand..." he sighed as he pulled me into a hug...

"You do?"

"Yes..."

"Thank you..."

"You don't have to thank me..."

"The doctor's office is around the corner from Rockefeller Center..."

"That's nice..."

"We can go to the doctor and then we can spend the day together..."

"I'd like that..."

"Let me go – Billy will wind up being late..." I said as I pulled away from him and went downstairs...

"Billy?"

"I'm ready Mommy..."

"You're ready? Oh wow..."

"I got up early..."

"Okay – I'm going to go back upstairs and get dressed...

"Good morning Daddy..."

"Good morning Billy..." William went into the kitchen and turned on the kettle to make me coffee. Billy turned on the tv..."

"I took the pregnancy test last night..."

"How'd he react?"

"He's thrilled..."

"This doesn't change anything – right?'

"Nothing's changed..."

"Call me when you get in the car..."

"Okay..."

"I'll see you tonight..." I said as I pulled William into a kiss..."

"See you tonight – I love you..."

"I love you too..."

"Bye Daddy – I love you..."

"I love you too Billy..." I dropped Billy off at school before I called Dante...

"Hey..."

"Hey..."

"You're still leaving him – right?"

"Yes Dante..."

"You said he was thrilled..."

"He is..."

"I hope this doesn't back fire on us..."

"It won't..."

"You seem so sure..."

"He's so happy he'll do anything I want..."

"I don't want to lose you..."

"You're not going to lose me Dante..."

"Can I see you tonight?'

"No..."

"See? I knew it..."

"Dante – I told William I started a new project at work and I'll be staying late one to two days a week..."

"So why can't I see you tonight?"

"Because we have to be careful – and I don't want to have dinner with Dawn again..."

"I'm sorry..."

"That's okay..."

"I still wanna see you though..."

"I'll see you tomorrow..."

"You promise?"

"Yes Dante..."

"I can't wait..."

"I told William I don't want him to tell Billy yet..."

"Because he'll tell Dawn..."

"Exactly..."

"I hope we can make this happen before you start showing..."

"I'm going to an OBGYN in midtown..."

"You are?"

"Yea..."

"Because you don't want to run into Dawn..."

"Yea..."

"I hate that you have to jump through hoops like this..."

"So do I – I told William that since it's around the corner from Rockefeller Center, we can make a day of it..."

"So you're going to be on a romantic date..."

"Yea..."

"I hate this shit..."

"I'm sorry Dante – I don't have a choice..."

"I know – I need to go – I'll talk to you later..."

"I'm sorry Dante..." I said as I called to make an appointment with Dr. Perera...

"Dr. Perara's office – how may I help you?"

"I'd like to make an appointment..."

"Are you a new patient?"

"Yes..."

"What insurance do you have?"

"Blue Cross..."

"Okay – we had a cancellation for this morning at 11:30 – would you like that?"

"Yes..."

"Okay – may I have your name?"

"Demi Taylor..."

"Date of birth?"

"4/6/86..."

"Hmm – you're in our system – are you a patient of Dr. Dunn?"

"Yes..."

"Why do you need to see Dr. Perera?"

"Dr. Dunn doesn't deliver babies anymore..."

"Oh you're pregnant – okay – congratulations – make sure you bring your insurance card with you..."

"Okay – thank you..."

"Hey..." William answered..."

"I need you to meet me at 51 West 51st Street at 11:30..."

"What's wrong?"

"Nothing – I got an appointment to see Dr. Perera..."

"Dr. Perera?"

"She's an OBGYN..."

"I'll be there..."

"I'll see you there – I need to go into work..."

"Hey..."
"Hey Dawn..."
"We need to make this quick..." she said as she headed upstairs..."
"Since when?"
"Since I have a doctor's appointment at 11..." she answered as she got undressed...

"Can I use the bathroom?"
"Sure..."
"Thanks..." she said as she got up out the bed and went into the bathroom. Her eyes got wide and her mouth dropped open when she saw the pregnancy test on the sink... "Shit! Shit! Shit! Shit! Shit!"
"What's wrong?! William exclaimed as he hurried into the bathroom... "Oh..."
"When did you find out?"
"Last night..."
"Congratulations..."
"Don't say anything..."
"Why?"
"Because we haven't told Billy yet..."
"Okay..." she said as she took out a clean wash cloth. William waited for her to freshen up and get dressed and then they both went downstairs... "I'll see you later tonight..."
"See you tonight..." They both got in their cars and drove off...

"GOD DAMMIT!" she exclaimed... "Why the fuck does she have to be pregnant now?! Just what the fuck I need – I can already see it – they'll be one big happy family and I'll be pushed to the side! That's okay – I'm going to the doctor – I just know I'm pregnant – I know Dante doesn't want kids but I'll get him to change his mind – we can be happy – he'll see..."

"Good morning - how may I help you?"

"I'm here to see Dr. Perera..." I answered...

"Excuse me – where's your bathroom?" William asked...

"Down the hall to the right..."

"Dawn Taylor?" I heard. I froze...

"Yes?" I heard her answer...

"Dr. Kim is ready for you..." I heard the woman say...

"Excuse me – you said you had an appointment?"

"Oh – yes – sorry – I'm here for Dr. Perera..."

"Name please?"

"Demi Taylor..."

"Did you bring your insurance card with you?"

"Yes..." I answered as I handed her my card...

"You're all set –have a seat – the Dr. will call you shortly..." I sat down and took out my phone...

"911!"
"What's wrong?!"
"Dawn is here!"
"Where?"
"At the OBGYN!"
"WHAT?!"
"Williams coming – ttyl."

"Hey..." I sighed as he sat down..."
"Demi Taylor?"
"Yes?" we both answered...
"The doctor is ready for you..." We both got up and started down the hall... "Are you any relation to Dawn Taylor?"
"Did you say Dawn Taylor?" William asked...
"Yes..."
"No relation..." I answered as we went into the exam room...

"You're all set..." Dr. Kim said...
"Thank you doctor..."
"I'll see you next month..."
"I can't wait to tell Dante I'm pregnant..." she sighed as she hugged the sonogram...

"Are you a patient of Dr. Dunn?"
"Yes..."

"Why are you here to see me?"

"Because she doesn't deliver babies anymore..." William answered...

"I see – congratulations..."

"Thank you..."

"I'll start with an exam, we'll do a sonogram, and we'll take it from there..."

"Okay..."

"I need you to get undressed, put the gown on –you know the drill – I'll be right back..."

"Let me help you..." William said as he came over to me and began to unbutton my blouse...

"William – stop it!" I laughed...

"Okay – hurry up!" He was so happy. I started feeling guilty...

"Why do I do this to myself?" I thought as the doctor came in...

"C'mon..." she said as she patted the table. I got up on the table, opened my legs, and put my feet in the stirrups... "Scoot down... Ready?"

"Yea..." William was more ready than I was...

"Is she okay?"

"Ask her..." Dr. Perera laughed...

"I mean – does everything look okay..."

"Yes – everything looks good – is this your first?"

"Yes – No..."

"Okay – which is it?" she laughed...

"It's my first – his second..."

"She's my first girl..." William sighed...

"Okay – I'll do a sonogram..." she said as she turned on the machine... "Ready?"

"Ready..." we both answered...

"This will be cold..." she said as she squirted the jelly on me...

"It's not that bad..." I said. Dr. Perera started the sonogram and we saw our baby...

"Hello Demi..." he whispered as he took my hand. He started crying and I couldn't hold back the tears...

"That's our baby..." he whispered...

"That's our baby..." I whispered. Dr. Perera took out her camera and took a picture of us...

"This is beautiful..." she sighed. I'll send it to your phone. William continued to hold my hand as she went over my abdomen...

"She's beautiful..." he cried. I was still crying too...

"I'll print you out a few pictures..." She printed out the pictures and handed them to William...

"I love you so much..."

"I love you too..."

"You can get dressed – I'll be right back..." William helped me sit up and held me as we both continued crying. He had no idea I was crying for a different reason...

"Can I come in?"

"Yes..." William answered...

"Umm – you're not dressed..." she laughed...

"I'm sorry..."

"I'll see you in four weeks..." she said as she started to leave...

"Umm – Dr. Perera?"

"Yes?"

"How far along is she?"

"After looking at the fetus – I'd say she's about eight weeks..."

"Spend the rest of the day with me..."

"I can't – I need to pick Billy up from school..."

"His mother can pick him up from school..."

"What about his homework?"

"She can take him home – she can help him with his homework – we can pick him up on our way home..."

"Okay..." I agreed as I connected my phone to my car..."

"Hello Demi..."

"Hello Dawn – could you pick Billy up from school?"

"Sure – is everything alright?"

"Everything's fine – I'm out to lunch with William – we won't be back in time..."

"What time do you think you'll be back?"

"I'm not sure – could you take Billy home? We'll pick him up on the way back..."

"You don't have my address..."

"I will when you text it to me..."

"Fine – I'll text you the address...

"Thanks – we'll see you later..."

We went by Rockefeller Center, we went ice skating, we went to see a show in Radio City Music Hall, and then we went to dinner... "I'm sorry..."

"For what?"

"Everything..." he answered as he picked up my hand and kissed it...

"Hey Dawn – Hey Billy!"

"Hi Dante..." Billy greeted...

"I'm surprised to see you here on a school night..."

"Demi asked me to pick him up from school..."

"Oh – what time are they coming to pick him up?"

"I don't know – I hope it's not too late though..."

"Why?"

"Billy – go inside – I'll be there in a minute..."

"Okay Mommy..." Dante waited for Billy to go down the hall...

"What's going on Dawn?"

"I have something to tell you..." she said as she took his hands...

"What do you need to tell me?"

"Dante... I'm pregnant..."

"Pregnant? Wow!"

"I know you said you don't want kids but here..." she said as she opened her purse and took out the sonogram...

"Is that the baby?"

"Yes Dante..."

"Hmmm – look at that..."

"Are you upset?"

"I'm okay – I just need time to process this..."

"Okay – I understand – I'll give you time..."

"Go help Billy with his homework – I need time to think..."

"Okay..."

"William – we need to..."

"Come with me..." he said as he pulled me across the street to the Hilton...

"Welcome to the Hilton – can I get you a room?"

"Yes... William answered as he pulled out his American Express..."

"Hmmm – right now we only have a Double Queen – is that alright?"

"That's fine..."

"Here you go Mr. Taylor – you're in room 515..."

"Thank you..." he breathed as he pulled me towards the elevator...

"Mommy?"

"Yes Billy?"

"When is Mommy coming to get me?"

"Soon..."

"Okay..."

"Mmmph...   Mmmph...   Mmmph... Mmmph..."

"Mmm... Mmm... Mmm... Mmm..."

"Mmmph...   Mmmph...   Mmmph... Mmmph..."

"Mmm... Mmm... Mmm... Mmm..."

"Mmmph! Mmmph! Mmmph! Mmmph!"

"Mmm! Mmm! Mmm! Mmm!"

"I love you so much..."

"William – I..."

"Don't talk – just let me love you..." he breathed as he kissed me again...

"It's 8pm – Billy's bedtime is 9pm – where are you?!"

"What's that?" William asked...

"It's a text from Dawn..."

"Tell her we're on our way..."

"We're on our way..."

"On your way from where?!"

I ignored her text – and then I got another one from Dante...

"She's pregnant!"

"I'm sorry..."

"I need to see you..."

"I'll see you tomorrow night..."

"Make it tomorrow morning..."

"Okay..."

"Mommy! Daddy!" Billy exclaimed...

"Bout time you got here..." Dawn said...

"Hello William, hello Demi..."

"Hello Dante – sorry I kept my wife out so late – I had to make up for lost time..."

"It's fine..."

"C'mon Billy – it's past your bedtime..."

"Bye Mommy! Bye Dante!"

"Good night..." they both said...

"Dante – can we talk?"

"Not tonight – I need time to think..."

"Where did you go Daddy?"

"I took your mother out to dinner..."

"Oh..." We rode in silence. Billy fell asleep in the back seat...

"C'mon Billy..." William said as he lifted Billy out the back seat. I unlocked the door, I held it open, he brought Billy into the house, and carried him into his room... "I'm glad his room is downstairs..." he laughed...

"I'm going upstairs..." I yawned...

"I'll be up in a minute..." I got undressed, got in bed, and closed my eyes. I was asleep before he got upstairs...

"Sleep well... I love you both..." he whispered.

"*I*'m tired..."

"I know Billy – I'm sorry..." I got him dressed and we started to leave...

"Excuse me?"

"I'm sorry..." I said as I went to kiss William. Billy followed me and hugged him around his leg...

"I love you Daddy..."

"I love you too – and I love you both..." he breathed as he kissed me...

"I love you too..." I said as I took Billy outside...

"Mommy – what's wrong?"

"Nothing – I'm just tired..."

"Oh..." I was happy he didn't ask me any more questions... "Have a good day Mommy – I love you..."

"I love you too..." I connected my phone to the car as soon as I pulled off...

"Are you on your way?'
"Yes..."
"Good..."
"You sound like you're upset with me..."
"Should I be?'
"Dante – what's wrong?"
"I'll talk to you when you get here..."

"I can't stay long Dante..." I started to say as he opened the door...
"He has a tracker on your car – I know..." he interrupted...
"Dante... What's wrong?"
"You tell me..."
"I don't understand..."
"You spent the whole day with him – he's happy about the baby – and so are you..."
"Yes..."
"So you're staying with him?"
"Dante..."
"It's a yes or no question..."
"I want to be with you... but yesterday... we saw the baby... we cried..."
"And he took you to dinner, he took you to a hotel, and he fucked you..."
"Dante!"
"Am I wrong?"
"No..." I sighed...
"You're torn now – aren't you?"

"Yes..."

"I knew this was going to happen..."

"Dante – I'm sorry – I love you – but I love him too – and we're having a baby..."

"So you've decided to keep the baby?"

"Yes..."

"You know I'm not helping you raise that mutha fucka's child..."

"Yes..."

"So what – I'm supposed to just keep fucking you for nine months?"

"Seven..."

"Seven? You're eight weeks pregnant?"

"Yes..."

"Hmmm – so is she..."

"I thought you didn't want any kids?"

"I don't want any kids – and I'm not having any..."

"So you're going to tell Dawn to get an abortion?"

"Come sit down..." I went to sit down. He sat down beside me... "You know I love you – right?"

"Yes Dante..."

"I'll always love you – even if you decide you want to be with William, have his baby, and try to make your marriage work..."

"So this is good bye?" I asked as I teared up...

"That's up to you – but... Damn... I wish I didn't have to do this..."

"Are you trying to tell me you don't want to see me again?"

"Demi... this is really hard... I need you to listen..."

"Okay..."

"Dawn is eight weeks pregnant..."

"Okay..."

"I had a vasectomy two years ago..."

"You had a vasectomy two years ago?!"

"Yes..."

"No... No... No... No..." I said as I shook my head back and forth...

"Demi..."

"IT'S NOT TRUE!" I exclaimed as I started crying...

"Demi... I'm sorry..."

"It can't be true... he wouldn't do that to me – would he?"

"Yes..."

"So they've both been making a fool of me..."

"Dawn doesn't know..."

"YES SHE DOES!" I cried...

"I never told Dawn I got a vasectomy..."

"So she thinks she's pregnant by you?"

"Yes..."

"I can't believe I wanted to try and make our marriage work..."

"You love your husband..."

"I love him but he doesn't love anybody but himself..."

"Are you going to leave him now?"

"No..."

"Okay..." he sighed... "I understand..."

"No you don't..."

"I don't?"

"I'm going to file for a divorce..."

"Are you serious?"

"Yes I am..."

"Are you going to tell him he has a child on the way with her?"

"Nope..."

"Oh wow..."

"He'll find out he has a child on the way with her after you tell her you had a vasectomy two years ago..."

"You want me to tell her?!"

"That has nothing to do with me..."

"I'll tell her tonight..."

"You will?"

"Yes..."

"I can't wait..." I said as I smiled mischievously...

"Can I still see you tonight?"

"No..." I answered as I stood up... "But you can take me in your bedroom and see me now..." Dante stood up, picked me up in his arms, and carried me into their bedroom...

I went to work in a daze... "You look like you need coffee..." Annette said...

"Good morning to you too..." I responded...

"Here..."

"Thank you girl..."

"You're welcome..." I spent the rest of the day tied to my desk. I didn't even break for lunch

– I order off Uber Eats, brought it back to my desk, and continued working as I ate...

"I see what you're doing..." my manger said...

"What am I doing?"

"Working through lunch..."

"I'm not working – I'm on Amazon..." I laughed...

"Oh – okay..." I took out my phone and sent Dante a text...

"I wish you wanted kids and this was your baby..."

"Hi Mommy!" Billy exclaimed...

"Hey – come sit down – I have something to tell you..." Dawn said as she sat on the couch. William sat down too...

"Yes Mommy?"

"You're going to be a big brother..." William looked at her in shock...

"I am?!"

"Yes Billy – Mommy's having a baby..."

"Yeeaaa!" he exclaimed as he hugged her...

"Hey..." I greeted as I walked in...

"Mommy – guess what – I'm gonna be a big brother!"

"You are?!"

"Yes – Mommy's having a baby!"

"I need to lie down..." I said as I went upstairs...

"C'mon Billy – let's do your homework..."

As soon as I got upstairs, I sat down and sent Dante a text...

"Dawn just told Billy she was having a baby!"

"What?!"

"I'm so fuckin' pissed!"

"I'm sorry..."

"William and I decided to wait because I didn't want her to know about me – we didn't want her to tell him – I swear to God – if I didn't know better – I'd swear she did this on purpose!"

"Do you think she knows you're pregnant?"

"Oh God – I hope not – I swear – if I find out he told her..."

"I don't think he'd do that..."

"Yea – he wouldn't do that..."

I didn't go back downstairs. William brought me up a sandwich... "Thank you..."

"You're welcome..."

"She did that on purpose..." I said as I took a bite...

"No she didn't..."

"Yes she did..."

"Okay – what if she did?"

"I don't want to be pregnant with her – it's bad enough we have the same doctor..."

"How do you know that?" he asked as he looked at me...

"The technician asked me if I was any relation to Dawn Taylor – remember?"

"That doesn't mean you have the same doctor..."

"We have the same doctor..."

"Why would you think that?"

"Because I saw her..."

"You saw her? Why didn't you tell me?"

"Why would I tell you?" We were so happy – I didn't want to share that moment with her – we're already sharing you and her child..."

"Okay – that's enough – you don't need to be stressed..." he said as he walked over to me and began to massage my shoulders...

"Hey Dante..."

"Hey..."

"I have something to tell you..."

"I have something to tell you too..."

"I told Billy he was going to be a big brother..."

"Why would you tell him that when I'm still trying to process this?"

"Give it time Dante – you'll come around..."

"You still shouldn't've told Billy you were pregnant..."

"Why?"

"Dawn – I had a vasectomy two years ago..."

"You... had... a vasectomy?"

"Yea – so you might be pregnant – BUT YOUR'E NOT PREGNANT BY ME!" he gritted as he grabbed his jacket, grabbed his keys, and slammed the door shut.

I got up and shut off the alarm... "Stay – I'll get Billy..."

"Oh no..." I said as I jumped up and ran to the bathroom...

"Are you okay?"

"Yea..."

"I'll get Billy ready..." he said as he went downstairs. I took a shower, got dressed, and went downstairs...

"Good morning Mommy..."

"Good morning – Honey – could you make me some coffee?"

"Are you sure you should be drinking coffee?"

"Yes William..."

"Are you sick Mommy?"

"No Billy..."

"Okay..." William handed me the coffee and I sipped it. They both looked at me as I sipped...

"Okay Billy – it's time to go..." I said as I got up...

"Bye Daddy..."

"Bye Honey..." I said as I gave him a quick kiss...

"Mmm – coffee lips..."

"Well see you later..." I laughed as we left...

"Mommy – your phone is ringing..."

"Can you see who it is?"

"It says Dante..."

"Could you answer it?"

"Hi Dante..."

"Hello Billy – are you on your way to school?"

"Yes..."

"Oh okay – have a nice day..." Dante said as he hung up...

"That was nice..." I sighed...

"Bye Mommy!" he said as he got out...

"Bye..." I connected my phone to the car and called him back...

"I'm sorry..."

"Don't worry about it – what's wrong?"

"I left her..."

"You left her?!"

"I couldn't take it anymore – she told Billy she was having a baby – I told her I needed more time before we told him – she tells me I'll get used to it..."

"So she basically made up her mind..."

"Yes she did – so I made up mine – I told her I had a vasectomy two years ago so she might be pregnant – but she's not pregnant by me!"

"WOW!"

"I'm sorry – I just couldn't take another second!"

"I'm sorry..."

"You don't need to apologize..."

"Yes I do..."

"Why do you think you need to apologize to me?"

"Because I've only been thinking about how hard this is for me..."

"You know I love you – right?"

"Yes..."

"I don't wanna go back..."

"Where are you staying?"

"I'm at the Marriott..."

"Okay – I just pulled into the parking lot – I'll call you later..."

"Could you make that call in person?"

"I'll let you know..."

"Hey..." Dawn sighed...

"What's wrong?"

"Please don't hate me..."

"Because you told Billy you're having a baby?"

"No..." she answered as she sat down...

"What's going on?" he asked as he sat down...

"I told Dante I was pregnant..."

"He doesn't want the baby?"

"He told me he had a vasectomy two years ago..."

"Are you telling me you're having my baby?!"

"Yes..."

"Get rid of it..."

"WHAT?!"

"Get rid of it..."

"Are you telling your wife to get rid of her baby?!"

"GET THE FUCK OUT!" he gritted as he snatched her up by the arm...

"William – I'm sorry!" William responded by opening the door and throwing her out...

"FFFUUUCCCKKK!!!"

"Hey..." I sighed...

"Hi Mommy – what's wrong?"

"I had a long day..." I answered...

"Come here..." William said as he pulled me into a hug...

"Dawn – you can go help Billy with his homework – I'm so tired..." I said as I sat down...

"I don't need your permission to help my son with his homework..."

"Dawn – I'm not in the mood – I'm tired – would you please just go inside?"

"I'll go inside when I'm good and ready!"

"Dawn – stop it..." William said

"What am I doing?!"

"Look – are you helping Billy with his homework or not? Isn't that why you're here?!" I snapped...

"Why else would I be here?! I'm not here to see you!"

"You're not helping Billy either – gee – I wonder why?!"

"Dawn – if you're not going to help Billy with his homework – leave..." William said...

"Unfuckinbelievable..." she mumbled as she went into Billy's room...

"BILLY! WAKE UP!" William beat me to it...

"BILLY! WAKE UP!"

"WHAT'S WRONG?!" I cried as I ran into his room...

"CALL 911!" Dawn screamed...

"911 – What's your emergency?"

"MY SON – HE WON'T WAKE UP!"

"Is he breathing?"

"I DON'T KNOW!"

"Maam – help is on the way – what's your name?"

"Demi..."

"Demi – can you tell me what happened?"

"He... William... Here..." I cried as I turned to hand him the phone. He was standing there crying, holding Billy in his arms... "NNNOOOO!"

"OPEN THE DOOR!" Dawn snatched the door open and the paramedics went to take Billy...

"Sir – let us take him..." William allowed him to take Billy and the paramedic carried him out to the stretcher. I didn't notice a 2nd paramedic coming out of his room...

"Did you give your son Tylenol?" We all turned around...

"No..." William answered...

"This was in his bed..." the paramedic said as he went outside...

"I'm riding in the ambulance..." Dawn said. I didn't care – I just wanted to comfort William...

"C'mon – I'll drive..." I said as we got in the car...

"We have an overdose!" the paramedic yelled as they pushed Billy inside. We all followed them...

"You all can't be in here!" the doctor snapped...

"We're his parents!" I snapped...

"WE'RE HIS PARENTS!" Dawn exclaimed as she pointed to the two of them...

"I'll be outside..." I said as I turned to leave. As soon as I found a chair, I took out my phone...

"We're at Saint Vincent's..."

"What happened?"

"Billy overdosed..."

"I'm on my way..."

"Billy..."
"Where am I?"
"Come to the light..."
"Aiden? Is that you?"
"Yes! C'mon!" Billy ran towards the light and Aiden pulled him through it... "Hey!" he exclaimed as he pulled Billy into a hug...
"Hey Aiden! Where am I?"
"You're in Heaven..."
"I'm in Heaven?"
"Yes! C'mon! Your other friends are here!" he exclaimed as he took Billy by the hand and pulled him towards the clouds...
"Hey Billy!" they all exclaimed...
"Hey! I'm so happy to see you guys!"
"We're happy to see you too!"
"Why are you here?" Billy asked...
"My parents got divorced..." Aiden answered...
"I thought you got transferred to another school..."
"I know – my parents didn't want anybody to know..."
"My parents wouldn't stop fighting..."
"We know..."
"You do? How?"
"We've been watching over you..."
"You have?!"
"Yes – and now that you're here – you'll be watching over everybody too..."
"Will I ever see my parents again?"

"We'll all see our parents again – and when we see them – they'll be happy..."

"They will?!"

"Yes – everybody's happy here..."

"So we're all one big happy family?"

"Yes..." Billy smiled and his smile lit up the clouds along with all the other children...

"Demi..."

"Oh God..." I cried as I fell into his arms...

"Dante..." Dawn cried as she ran over to us. I turned to look at William and I knew...

"NNNOOO!" I cried as I ran to him. He broke down and it broke my heart...

"This is my fault..."

"No it's not..."

"Mr. Taylor?" We turned to look at the doctor... "Would you like to see your son one last time before we do an autopsy?"

"Why do you need to do an autopsy? You already know how he died!"

"I'm sorry... the law requires it..."

"I'd like to see him..." I said...

"You're not his mother..." Dawn said...

"BITCH – SHUT THE FUCK UP!" William growled...

"I'm leaving..." Dante said...

"Dante – don't leave – stay with me – they can go..." I sighed...

"Are you sure you want me to stay?"

"Yes..." William turned to go with the doctor and Dawn stood there looking at us...

"Are you coming or not?!" Dawn turned to go and they both followed the doctor...

"I shouldn't be here..."

"I'm glad you're here..."

"You're going back to him – aren't you?"

"I have to..."

"Don't ever say that to me again – I'm tired of hearing it..."

"I'm sorry..."

"I'm sorry too..." he said as he got up...

"Where are you going?"

"I'm going back to the hotel..." he said as he got up. I sat there and cried as he left...

"Demi..." I looked up and William was standing in front of me. He held out his hand, I took it, he helped me up, and we walked to the car...

"I need a ride..." Dawn said...

"That's not my problem..." I said as I unlocked the car...

"William!" she exclaimed. William got in the car with me, we locked the doors, and I drove off.

"*H*ow long have you been cheating on me?" he asked as we sat down...

"Not as long as you've been cheating on me..."

"I'm sorry..."

"Save it..."

"Can we start over?"

"I don't think so..."

"You're pregnant..."

"Yes I am..."

"We have a second chance..."

"Dawn is pregnant too..."

"I told her to get rid of it..."

"Oh my God – you are so fuckin' delusional – you think because you told Dawn to have an abortion we can live happily ever after?"

"I don't want a baby with her – I don't want anything to do with her – I want you..."

"You want us both... and Billy suffered the consequences..."

"I never meant to hurt my son..."

"That bitch made it clear I wasn't his mother – I'm done with her – I'm done with this toxic polyamory marriage – I want out..." I said as I pushed him away from me. William looked at me and I saw rage. I knew what was coming and I didn't give a fuck. It was finally out and I was relieved...

"I'll kill you before I let you leave me..." he gritted as he grabbed my throat and began squeezing...

"Kill... Me... Take... Me... Out... As... Long... As... I'm... Free..."

"I'm sorry..." he sighed as he stopped squeezing. I started coughing uncontrollably and he tried to pat my back...

"DON'T!" I exclaimed as I got up and opened the door...

"Demi... I'm sorry..."

"Bitch – move..." I said as I pushed past Dawn and went to get in the car...

"Who is it?"

"Me..." Dante didn't open the door right away... "Dante..."

"Go away..."

"Dante... Please..." He got up and opened the door...

"Why are you here?"

"Can I come in? Please?" I sighed with relief as he opened the door wider and let me in...

"Why aren't you with your husband?" he asked as he closed the door and turned on the light... "Oh my God..." he whispered when he saw my neck. He pulled me into his arms and I sobbed. He let me cry for a while until I stopped... "Come sit..." I went to sit on the chaise lounge and he sat down with me...

"It's over..."

"You came here to break up with me?!"

"No Dante – I came here to tell you my marriage is over. I'm done with William for good..."

"You said that before – how do I know you really mean it?"

"Because I told him I was done with Dawn – with him – and our toxic polyamory marriage..."

"You're still pregnant..."

"So is Dawn..."

"I know..."

"He actually believed we could start over because he told her to have an abortion..."

"He told you that?!"

"Yes..."

"What the fuck is wrong with him?!"

"I don't care anymore..." I sighed...

"I thought I lost you..."

"I'm sorry..."

"You don't need to apologize..."

"Yes I do..."

"I knew what it was from the beginning but I didn't care – I wanted you in spite of it..."

"Make love to me..." Dante got up, helped me up, and took me to bed...

"Demi..."

"Huh?"

"Your phone is ringing..." Dante said as he handed it to me...

"Good morning..."

"Mrs. Taylor?"

"This is Mrs. Taylor..."

"This is Ms. Anderson..."

"Hello Ms. Anderson..."

"I'm calling you because Billy isn't here..."

"Billy died last night..."

"Oh my God! I'm so sorry!"

"Thank you..."

"Is there anything I can do?"

"Yes – you can call his father from now on..." I said as I hung up...

"Damn – that was harsh..." Dante said as I got up...

"I'll go apologize later..." I said as I dialed Annette's number...

"Hey Girl..."

"Hey Annette – I won't be in for the rest of the week – I'm taking Bereavement – my son died..."

"Oh no! I'm so sorry..."

"Thank you – I need to go..." I said as I teared up. Dante held me and I sobbed...

"Hey..." William sighed as he let Dawn in...

"I can't believe he's gone..." she whispered as she started crying...

"I've been working on the arrangements..."

"I'm not ready..."

"I have an appointment with Lester Gee Funeral Home at 11 – would you like to go with me?"

"Yes..."

"Okay..." William went into the kitchen to make coffee and Dawn went into Billy's room...

"Oh Billy..." she cried as she curled up on his bed and sobbed. William came into the room, sat on the bed, and pulled her into his arms... "I'M SORRY!" she screamed...

"C'mon – you need to eat..."

"I can't... I have too much to do..."

"You don't need to do anything but let me take care of you..."

"I loved him..."

"I know..."

"You told me he wasn't happy – I should've..."

"NO!"

"Dante..."

"DON'T YOU DARE BLAME YOURSELF!"

"But Dante..."

"STOP IT!" he gritted as he kissed me hard...

"Okay..."

"Okay —now I'm going to order room service and we're going to eat breakfast – okay?" I nodded in agreement and wiped my eyes. Dante picked up the phone to order room service and I picked up my phone... "Hello – I'd like to order breakfast... Uh Huh... Yes I'd like that... I'll take that too... Yes please... Thank you..."

"Sounds like you ordered a lot of food..."

"What are you doing?"

"I'm scheduling an appointment with Planned Parenthood..."

"I thought I made myself clear..." he said as he took my phone out my hand...

"Dante... I...."

"Not today..." he said as he put my phone in his pocket...

"William... Please..."

"You want me to make love to you?"

"Yes... but..."

"What's wrong?"

"I don't want to have an abortion... I wanna keep my baby..."

"Our baby..." he breathed as he kissed her..."

"Our baby? You mean it?"

"Yes..."

"Oh William..."

"Who is it?"

"Room Service..." Dante got up to answer the door...

"Thank you..."

"You're welcome – have a good day..." I started to get out of bed and he stopped me... "Stay there..."

"Okay..." I watched him make two plates of food and put them on the food tray...

"Are you coming back to bed?"

"Yes..." I smiled as he put the tray over my lap. He made two cups of coffee, put them on the tray, and got back in bed beside me...

"That looks good..."

"Eat..." he commanded as he put some eggs on the fork and held it to my mouth...

"Can I ask you something?"

"Yes..."

"What about Demi?"

"What about her?"

"How will she feel about me having another baby with you?"

"I don't care..." he breathed as he kissed her...

"Did you enjoy your breakfast?"

"Yes..."

"Do you feel better?"

"Yes... and No..."

"I know..."

"I can't believe he's gone..."

"I'm sorry..."

"I love you..."

"I love you too..."

"I'm here in a hotel with you – and I'm mourning his child..."

"He was your child too..."

"Yes he was..."

"If you could do anything you wanted right now – what would you do?"

"Anything?"

"Anything..."

"I'd go back to sleep, wake up, and be thankful that this was all a bad dream..."

"Would you still be with me?"

"Yes..."

"Are you sure you'd still be with me?"

"Dante – even if I went back to William – between him and Dawn – are marriage wasn't going to work..." Dante snuggled up next to me and smiled.

"I'm Lester Gee – sorry for your loss..."

"Thank you – I'm William Taylor and this is his mother, Dawn..."

"Nice meeting you – we'll do everything we can to make this process simple – do you have an obituary?"

"I have one..." Dawn answered as she handed him the paper...

"When did you write that?" William asked...

"I wrote it earlier..."

"Can I read it?"

"Sure..." Mr. Gee answered as he handed it to William...

"William Taylor, Jr., affectionately known as Billy, was born to William and Dawn Taylor on

February 10, 2016, in New Haven Hospital, New Haven, CT. He died on Sunday, January 28, 2024. He was 7 years old. Billy was a sweet, loving little boy. He was loved by his parents, his teachers, and his classmates. Billy attended Orange Avenue Elementary School in Milford, CT. He was a Straight-A student and his teachers had nothing but good things to say about him at teacher conferences. Billy loved his PS5. He would play games with his father and beat him often. Billy was an only child. He is survived by his father, William Taylor, Milford, CT, and his Mother, Dawn Taylor, Milford CT."

William picked up a pen and added something to the obituary... "What are you doing?" Dawn asked...

"I'm adding his step-mother..." he answered. Dawn was pissed but she didn't say anything. She picked up the paper and saw that William corrected the following...

"Billy was survived by his father, William Taylor, Milford, CT, his Mother, Dawn Taylor, Milford, CT, and his Step-Mother, Demi Taylor, Milford, CT."

"Any other changes?" Mr. Gee Asked...
"No..."
"Okay – we'll get this prepared – would you like a burial?"
"Yes..." they both answered...

"Come with me – I'll show you our selection..."

"Oh William..." Dawn whispered as she started crying. William teared up as he put his arm around her...

"Do you need a minute?' Mr. Gee asked...

"No – I want to see them...

"Okay..." he said as he led them into the room...

"William... they're so tiny... our baby..."

"Look..." he said as he pointed to the Titan Casket...

"I like it..." Dawn said...

"I have something else I'd like to show you..." Mr. Gee said as he motioned for them to follow him...

"That's the one..." William said as he walked up to the 'In God's Care Spruce Blue Casket with Blue Velvet Interior-Metal Casket...'

"In God's Care..." Dawn read...

"So you'll take it?"

"Yes..." William answered...

"Okay – I'll place the order for the casket..."

"How long will it take to get here?" William asked...

"It should be here by Thursday..."

"Should be?'

"Don't worry – if it's not here by Thursday we can use this one and replace it with the one you ordered..."

"Can we schedule the funeral for Friday?"

"Yes – we have Friday morning available..."

"Okay..."

"Alright – we'll get the paperwork processed and then we'll get your son here..."

"Thank you..."

Dante was snoring. I was happy he was still asleep. I eased out the bed, tip-toed over to the chaise lounge, and took my phone out his pocket. Dante didn't turn it off so I didn't have to worry about waking him. I went back to the internet and saw my search was still there for Planned Parenthood. I scrolled down to make the appointment and saw that the appointment I wanted for Monday wasn't available anymore... "Shit..." I whispered as I scrolled down to Tuesday... "9 a.m. – perfect!" I whispered as I booked the appointment...

"What are you doing?"

"I'm sorry... I..."

"Put the phone down..." I put the phone down... "Get in here..." I got back in the bed and snuggled up next to him... "I'm going to punish you..." he said as he started tickling me...

"Stop it!" I laughed...

"You don't listen – do you?!" he exclaimed as he tickled me...

"Okay-okay!" I laughed...

"Uh uh – I'm not finished!" he laughed as he kept tickling me. We both laughed as he continued to tickle me until my stomach hurt.

"Good morning..." he breathed as he kissed me awake...

"Good morning..." I breathed as I kissed him back. I tried to get up but he wasn't having it... "Dante... I need to pee..."

"If I let you up do you promise to come back to bed?"

"Dante – I have a lot to do..." I sighed...

"What do you have to do that's more important than me?"

"Okay – I'll come back to bed – I'll do you – and then we'll check out – okay?"

"Why do we need to check out? Why can't we have another day to just do us?"

"I'm going to pee – I'll come back to bed, I'll do you, and then we'll talk..."

"Okay..." I got up and went to the bathroom...

"Thank God I made that appointment..." I mumbled...

"Can we move Billy's room back upstairs?"

"Sure – when do you want to do that?"

"Can we do it today?"

"You want to do it today?"

"Yes..."

"Okay..." William sighed as he got up out the bed...

"Did you get the password to the computer downstairs?"

"KissMe24..."

"All caps?"

"Capital K, Capital M – the other letters are lower case – why?"

"I'm going to change it..."

"Why?"

"Demi doesn't need the password to our son's computer anymore..."

"Demi isn't here – and our son is dead..." he said as he went downstairs...

"Dante...   Dante...   Dante... DDDAAANNNTTTEEE!!!"

"I love the way you call my name when I fuck you..."

"I love the way you fuck me..."

"Oh yea?"

"Yea..."

"So why do you want us to check out?"

"We don't have to check out if you don't want to..."

"That's more like it..."

"But we need to talk..."

"Dammit!" he exclaimed as he sat up...

"I'm sorry..."

"You wanna talk – let's talk!"

"Please don't be mad at me!" I exclaimed as I started crying...

"I'm sorry..." he breathed as he pulled me into his arms... "We can talk if you want – we can do anything you want – please don't cry..."

"I want to go to your house..." I sniffed...

"You want us to check out and go to my house? Okay..."

"No..."

"What do you want?"

"I want to go to your house – I want to put Dawn's shit in garbage bags – I want to go to William's house – I want to open the door – and I want to throw the garbage bags inside!"

"Let's do it!" he exclaimed as he jumped up out the bed...

"I didn't realize how much stuff was in the office..." Dawn sighed...

"Demi added more things after she moved the office upstairs..."

"I'll be glad when she comes to get her things – I'll be glad when I can move in my things..."

"Let's pump the brakes..."

"Why?"

"We haven't even laid our son to rest and you're already planning to move in..."

"You don't want me to move in?"

"Let's just get these things downstairs..." he sighed...

"Where can I start?!" I exclaimed...

"You are really excited!"

"Damn right I am!" I exclaimed as I went into their bedroom...

"Demi – wait!"

"What am I waiting for?!" I exclaimed as I flung the closet door open... "I can't wait to put my things in here – I've always wanted a walk in closet!" I laughed as I opened the trash bag and began stuffing it with her clothes...

"That looks like fun – let me help you!" he laughed as he grabbed a garbage bag. We continued laughing as we stuffed the garbage bags. When we were done, there were 10 bags in the middle of the room...

"Wow – I'm tired..."

"Me too..."

"Does she have anything in the guest room?"

"She might..."

"What about the hall closet?"

"She might..."

"Okay – can we take a break and have breakfast? I've worked up an appetite..." Dante smiled at me mischievously...

"I'm going to take this desk apart and then I'll bring it downstairs..."

"William – why don't you leave it up here?"

"I wanted to bring the other desk up here..."

"The room downstairs is smaller – this desk actually fits up here better..."

"You're right – but don't you need a desk downstairs?"

"I can use the desk downstairs for now..."

"What about Billy's bed? Will his bed fit in here if we leave the desk in here?"

"His bed might not fit in here... but a new crib will..." William smiled as he went over to her and pulled her into a kiss...

"C'mon – we'll move all of Billy's things up here..."

"I don't think we should do that..."

"Why not?"

"I want to turn this room into a nursery for the baby – I don't want this room to be a memorial to Billy..."

"What should we do with Billy's things then?"

"I'll pack them up and bring them to the Rescue Mission..."

Dante made us coffee and sandwiches on Portuguese rolls. "Damn that was good..." I sighed...

"You're welcome..."

"I guess we can start in the guest room..." I sighed as I got up. We took the garbage bags, we went into the guest room, and I opened the closet door...

"Demi..." he sighed as he hurried over to me to comfort me. I took Billy's coat off the hanger and held it close to my chest as I cried... "Let's take a break..."

"No – I'll be okay..." I said as I stuffed Billy's coat in the bag. I saw a few more things that belonged to him and I stuffed them in the bag...

"Demi – Stop..." Dante said as he touched my shoulder...

"No – I'm okay..."

"No you're not..."

"I'll be okay Donte. We don't need Billy's things in here anymore..." I said as I continued to stuff the bag...

"I guess you're right..." he sighed as he emptied the dresser drawers...

"Oh look – Dawn had a few things in here too..." I said as I pulled her coats off the hangers. I looked in the bottom of the closet and saw a pair of Billy's sneakers... "I remember when we bought these..." I sighed. Dante was relieved when he saw me smile. I stuffed them in the bag along with a pair of her shoes...

"All we need to do now is clean out the hall closet and we're done..."

"*I* want Demi's new computer..."

"No..."

"Why not?"

"Because it's hers..."

"She only bought it because..."

"She bought it because she wanted Billy to have his own computer..."

"She just didn't want me on the same computer as her – she did that on purpose..."

"Billy is dead and you still don't get it..."

"That's not true..."

"I'm giving her the computer – you can continue to use Billy's computer – or you can buy yourself another one..."

"What if they're home?"

"That's even better..." I answered as I opened the door and threw the first bag inside...

"What the hell?!" William exclaimed as he ran downstairs. Dawn was right behind him...

"Demi!" William exclaimed...

"Hey!" I exclaimed as I threw another garbage bag inside...

"What the hell are you doing?!" Dawn exclaimed...

"I'm giving you your shit!" I exclaimed as I threw another garbage bag inside...

"Demi – stop it!" William exclaimed...

"You wanna help me? We have about 12 bags left!" I exclaimed as Dante got out the car...

"Dante?! How could you let her do this?!" Demi exclaimed. Dante ignored her and went around her...

"Hey William – where should I put these bags?"

"You can put them here – We'll go through them later..."

"Thanks man..." he said as he went back out to the car. They both watched us as we went back and forth... "You wanna get the last two bags?" Dante asked...

"Sure..." William answered as he got up and went to the car...

"How the fuck would you like it if I put all your shit in garbage bags and threw them down the fuckin' stairs?!" Demi exclaimed...

"SAY LESS!" I yelled as I stormed upstairs with a box of hefty garbage bags...

"William – don't just stand there – DO SOMETHING!"

"DANTE – COULD YOU COME HELP ME?!"

"COMING!" he answered as he started to get up...

"Stay here – I'll go help her..." William said as he blocked him from going up the stairs...

"I won't disrespect your house – but I'm going upstairs to help Demi get her things..." he said as he pushed William to the side...

"Over my dead body!" William gritted...

"We can make that happen!" Dante gritted...

"STOP IT!" Dawn exclaimed as they started tussling...

"WILLIAM!" I screamed from the top of the stairs. They both stopped and stood up... "HAVE YOU LOST YOUR GOT DAMNED MIND?!"

"I told him not to go upstairs..."

"FINE – SINCE YOU WANNA BE AN ASS – I'LL DO IT MYSELF! UUGGHHH!" I screamed as I started throwing bags downstairs...

"Enough of this shit!" Dante exclaimed as he ran up the stairs and into the bedroom... "Demi..."

"NO!"

"Demi – let me help you!"

"Okay –here!" I exclaimed as William came storming into the bedroom...

"I TOLD YOU NOT TO COME UPSTAIRS!" he boomed as he lunged towards Dante...

"LEAVE HIM ALONE!" I screamed as I got between them...

"DEMI – MOVE!"

"OR WHAT? YOU'LL THROW ME DOWN THE STAIRS AND KILL YOUR UNBORN CHILD?!" William froze. I gave Dante a bag and he went over to the closet...

"Is this stuff yours?"

"Yes..." William stepped aside and let us finish getting my things out the closet...

"Do you have anything in the bathroom?"

"Anything I left in the bathroom can be thrown away..."

"What about the dresser?"

"I have some things in the dresser..." I answered as I went over to the dresser. Dante waited for me to open the first drawer and came over to help me... "I have two more drawers..." William stood there and watched us. I took one final bag and swiped all of my things on the top of the dresser into it...

"Are you done?" Dante asked...

"We're done in here – I just need my things out of the office..."

"You can take the computer..." William said...

"I planned to..." I said as I followed Dante into the office. I saw that it was practically empty... "You're moving the office back downstairs..."

"Yes..."

"Hmmm..." I said as I disconnected the hard drive, the computer, and the printer. Dante put the printer in the box and took it downstairs...

"I'm sorry Demi..." William sighed...

"So am I..." I said as I picked up the computer, picked up the hard drive, and went downstairs... "Where's Dante?' I asked Dawn...

"He's putting your things in the car..." I took the computer out to the car and Dante turned around...

"Are we done?"

"I need to check the closet downstairs..."

"Okay..." We both came back inside and I gave Dante a bag...

"Where are you going?" Dawn asked...

"I'm going to get my things out the closet..." I answered as we went into Billy's room. Dante came over to me and held me as I teared up...

"Are you sure you wanna do this?"

"I'll be okay..." I sniffed as I pushed Billy's things out of the way and put my coats in the bag. William got up to see what we were doing...

"Are you okay?"

"She's okay..." Dante answered as he put his arm around me...

"Let's check the hall closet..." I sighed. We went to check the closet and I had a couple of coats, a pair of boots, and a pair of shoes in the bag...

"I have room in this bag..." Dante said...

"Is that everything?" Dawn asked...

"No – I still have one more thing..." I said as we took the bags out to the car. Dawn rolled her eyes and we went outside...

"What did you forget?'

"You're about to find out..." I answered as we went back inside... "Can we talk?" I asked as we sat down?"

"Sure..." William sighed. Dawn rolled her eyes...

"I moved Billy's room downstairs because Dawn was upstairs in our bedroom..."

"Do we have to do this now?" Dawn asked...

"Let her finish..." William said. Dante shook his head at me but I continued...

"In the process of moving Billy's room downstairs and moving the office upstairs, I found Dawn's manuscript..."

"I knew it!" she exclaimed...

"I started reading the manuscript and..."

"Tell me..." William said...

"Go ahead – tell him – he needs to know..." Dante added...

"No – William – I can explain..." Dawn interrupted...

"Tell me... please..." William pleaded....

"The title was 'My Worst Nightmare'..."

"You were using the computer in our office to write a book when you were supposed to be helping our son with is homework?"

"William – I can explain..."

"I decided to shred it after I read the first paragraph..."

"What did it say?"

"William – let me explain – please..."

"I thought I'd met the love of my life. Everything was fine as long as it went his way. I should warn her but fuck her – it's not like we're friends. She's lucky I'm cordial to her – but I guess I have to do that for my son. Every time I hear him call her Mommy it makes me cringe – and she eats it right up..."

"Oh my God – Demi – why didn't you tell me?"

"I found copies of her manuscript on the computer and I deleted them. She also left her email open and that's how I found out you were cheating on me..."

"It was you... You did all this..." Dawn said...

"No Dawn – you did all of this..." William corrected...

"Demi didn't know William was cheating on her with you until I showed her all your text messages..." Dante added...

"You were spying on me?"

"I wasn't spying on you – I was checking up on you – and when I went to T-Mobile, they helped me install a phone call tracker app – since your phone is under my account – I didn't need your permission – and the manager was more than willing to help me once I told him I suspected you were cheating on me..."

"Demi... I'm sorry... I had no idea..."

"I believe you..."

"You believe him?!" Dante exclaimed...

"I didn't know what Dawn was doing on the computer – and now that I know how she really feels about Demi – it all makes sense..."

"William – I can explain..."

"Don't bother – I should've checked you the first time you over-stepped your boundaries – if I had – Billy would still be alive – and my wife would be here with me right now instead of leaving with him..."

"Demi – are we done?" Dante asked...

"We're done..." I answered as I got up...

"GOOD BYE!" Dante exclaimed as he opened the door. I followed him out and we got in the car... "Was that really necessary?!" he snapped...

"Hell yea!"

"Let's go home..." he sighed...

"Wait a minute..."

"WHAT NOW?!" he exclaimed. I got out the car, unlocked the door, and went inside...

"What the hell do you want now?!" Dawn snapped...

"I wanted to return your key..." I answered as I took the key off my key ring and held it up for William to take. William took the key from me, I went outside, and I got back in the car...

"Are we finally done?!"

"Yes Dante..."

"So you don't have to come back here for anything?"

"No Dante..."

"Good!" he said as he started the car and drove off.

"Good morning..." Dante breathed as he kissed me...

"Good morning..." I yawned...

"Do you need to pee?"

"Yes..." I said as I got up...

"Will you come back to bed?"

"Dante – I have an appointment at 9 – and I need you to come with me..."

"Okay – can we take a shower first?"

"Yes – but that's all we're doing..."

"Huh... Huh... Huh..."

"Uggh! Uggh! Uggh!"

"Dante... I'm cumming..."

"I'm cumming with you..."

"HAAH! HAAH! HAAH! HAAH!"

"UGGH! UUGH! UUGH! UUGH!"

"We need to hurry up – I don't wanna be late..."

"What time is your appointment?"

"9..." I answered as I got out the shower and went to get dressed. Dante came out the bathroom and started getting dressed...

"You wanna tell me where we're going?"

"You'll see..." I sighed. Dante was going to push it but he thought it was best not to. I waited for him to get dressed and then we went downstairs...

"Can I get you some coffee?"

"What time is it?"

"It's 8:30..."

"We can get it to go..." Dante made us both coffee and we took it to the car... "What's the address?"

"35 Sixth Street..."

"Stamford?"

"Yea..."

"Welcome to Planned Parenthood – how may I help you?" the young lady asked. I looked around without answering... "Here ya go – just fill these out – my name's Ava – when you're done, bring them back to me – I'll make up a chart and someone will be out to see you..."

"Thank you Ava..." I said as I took the clipboard, looked at the forms, and started crying...

"You'll be alright..." Dante said as he comforted me. I filled out all the questions, went back to the counter, and gave Ava the clipboard...

"Someone will see you soon..." Ava said as she touched my hand to comfort me. I sat down and continued to cry. Dante put my head on his shoulder and rubbed my back...

"Demi Taylor?"

"Yes – I'm Demi Taylor..." I answered as we stood up...

"Come with me please..." she said as she motioned for us to follow her. We followed her down the hall and into an examination room... "Have a seat - My name's Carol..."

"Hi Carol..." I sniffed...

"I'm Mr. Taylor..." Dante lied...

"I've looked over your chart..."

"Okay..."

"You stated that you're here for an abortion..."

"Yes... that's correct..."

"Are you sure about this?"

"Yes..."

"You don't seem like you're sure..."

"My husband doesn't want the baby..." I sighed...

"Oh my God... I'm so sorry... Mr. Taylor – why don't you want your baby?"

"I never wanted children..."

"Mr. Taylor – could you excuse us for a minute?"

"You want me to stay?"

"I want him to stay..."

"Are you sure you don't want this baby?"

"It's not my baby..." Dante said...

"My husband knows it's not his baby because he can't have children..."

"Ohhhh... I see..."

"I don't want to have an abortion - but he told me he won't help me raise another man's child..."

"I'm so sorry..."

"It's okay – I just thank God he forgives me for cheating on him..."

"I forgive you... and I love you..." Dante breathed as he pulled me into a kiss...

"I love you too..."

"Wow – Okay - I'm going to take a urine sample, some blood, I'm gonna do a pelvic exam, and an ultrasound – we'll take it from there – you don't have to do anything today – okay?"

"Okay..."

"There's a cup in the bathroom – give me some urine, write your name on the cup, and come back in here..."

"Okay..." I got up and went to the bathroom. Thank God the bathroom was clean – a clean bathroom reduces my anxiety – especially when it comes to public bathrooms. After I peed in the cup, I wrote my name on it and went back to the room....

"Thanks..." Carol said as she took the urine from me... "Okay – I'm gonna take some blood now – have you eaten anything?"

"No..."

"Would you like some coffee?"

"No – I already had some – thank you..." I said as I watched her prepare the tubes and the needle...

"You okay?"

"Yes... I'm okay..."

"I always ask – some people don't like needles..." she said as she took my blood... "I'll be right back...

"She okay?" Ava asked...

"She's lucky..."

"What happened?"

"She's having an abortion because she cheated on him and that's not his baby!" she whispered...

"No! Is he mad?"

"He's a fool – she has him wrapped around her finger – he was just in there kissing her telling her that he loves her and he forgives her!"

"Damn she must have some bomb ass pussy!" Ava said as they both bust out laughing...

"I need to get back inside – I'll talk to you later...

"Okay – I'm going to do a pelvic exam – I need you to get undressed from the waist down – I'll leave if you want..."

"No – that's okay..." I said as I undressed and got back up on the table...

"Okay – scoot down a bit so we can see what's going on..." she said. I scooted down and she proceeded with a quick pelvic exam – by the time I felt her fingers inside me she was finished...

"Wow – that was quick..."

"Everything feels okay – now let's see how everything looks..." she said as she squirted the gel on my stomach, turned on the machine, and started doing the sonogram... "Hmmm..."

"Is everything okay?"

"It's hard to tell what's going on – I need to do a transvaginal ultrasound..."

"What's a transvaginal ultrasound?"

"I'm going to put this long tube in your vagina – it will help me see your uterus, fallopian tubes, ovaries, cervix, and your vagina..."

"Will it hurt?"

"No – it doesn't use radiation – you might feel a little discomfort as I'm putting the transducer in, but that's it..."

"Okay..."

"Are you ready?"

"Yes..."

"Take a deep breath... then relax..." she said as she put the transducer in my vagina... "Look... see that tiny little peanut right there?"

"Yes... I see it..."

"That's your baby..."

"I know..."

"Do you want a picture?"

"Yes..."

"Okay... I'll print one out for you..." she said as she printed the picture for me...

"Can I get up now?"

"Yes - I'm finished..." she answered as I started getting dressed...

"How far along is she?" Dante asked...

"She's about eight weeks..."

"Okay..."

"Okay – we've done the urine, the blood, the pelvic exam, the ultrasound. And the transvaginal ultrasound – now we need to talk about the abortion..."

"Okay..." I said as my eyes started tearing up. Dante took my hand and began rubbing my back...

"There are two categories of abortion..."

"Okay..."

"Medical is where we use medication that causes the uterus to expel the pregnancy. Surgical is where the clinician removes the pregnancy. The Medical Abortion uses a pill – it's similar to a miscarriage – you cramp, there's heavy bleeding, it can take longer, and requires more appointments..."

"Okay..."

"The Surgical Abortion feels more invasive, has more pain management, and is available quicker with fewer appointments. If you decide you want to go through with an abortion, you'll receive information on both procedures that explains the side effects and consequences. Before you get the abortion, both procedures require an education session and counseling..."

"I don't need education or counseling..." I said...

"It's mandatory..."

"You just counselled me..."

"Have you decided how you'd like to proceed?"

"Yes – I'll do the medical abortion..."

"Would you like to get the medication today?"

"Yes..."

"Okay – I'm going to give you the medication and I'm going to give you instructions. Please read them and make sure you follow them. If you have an emergency or any kind, you can call us 24-7..."

"Okay..."

"You'll need to stock up on maxi pads, food, etc., - and you'll need ibuprofen for the cramps – you can't take aspirin because that will make you bleed more..."

"Okay..."

"You're going to get two medications. The 1st one will stop the pregnancy from growing. The 2nd one will cause cramping, bleeding, and empty your uterus. You'll need to come back for a follow-up in two weeks..."

"Okay..."

"The cramping and bleeding will start between 1 and 4 hours. You may also spot and bleed for several weeks...."

"Okay..."

"Don't use tampons or a menstrual cup – use pads so you can keep track of your bleeding..."

"Okay..."

"You may also have tender breasts and they may leak a milky discharge. That should stop in a couple of days. Wearing a snug-fitting bra will help you feel more comfortable."

"Okay"

"Do you have any questions?"

"What happens when I come back for a follow-up?"

"You'll need to take a special pregnancy test called a low sensitivity pregnancy test to see if you're still pregnant..."

"I can still be pregnant?"

"For every pregnancy between 9 to 12 weeks – the chances are 2 in every 100."

"What do I do if that happens?"

"You need to have a surgical abortion..."

"Wait a minute – so if she's still pregnant in two weeks – she has to have a surgical abortion?"

"Yes – and it's important to take the test in two weeks because you won't be able to have an abortion after twelve weeks..."

"Oh my God..." I sighed...

"Let's not worry about that right now – I know I said 2 in every 100 – but that's only happened once since I've been working here – and I've been working here for ten years..."

"Okay..."

"So you still want to go through with the medical abortion?"

"Yes..."

"Okay..." she said as she handed me the medication... "Follow the instructions exactly –

and if you have any questions, if you're feeling nauseous, if you have a fever that lasts more than 24 hours, if you're feeling anxious – or if you just need to talk – call the 800 number..."

"Okay..."

"Do you have any other questions?"

"Yes..."

"Umm... How soon can I have sex again?"

"You can have sex whenever you feel ready..." Dante and I looked at each other and smiled...

"Thank you Carol..."

"You're welcome..." she said as she got up. Dante took my hand and walked me back towards the receptionist...

"Mrs. Taylor?"

"Yes Ava?"

"Can I speak with you a minute?"

"Sure – Dante can you go bring the car around to the entrance?"

"Sure – I'll be right back..."

"Yes Ava?" She motioned for me to come closer so she could whisper to me...

"I ain't tryin' to be all up in your business – but where you find him at?"

"I found him here in Stamford..." I laughed...

"Girl – how you get him to forgive you?"

"Forgive me?"

"Yea – for... you know..."

"Carol told you?"

"No – I read your chart..."

"It's in my chart?"

"Okay – I ain't gonna front – Carol told me you was a lucky woman..."

"So it's not in my chart?"

"No – the only thing in your chart is that you came in for an abortion and your husband gave his consent..."

"Okay..."

"So how you get him to forgive you?" This time I motioned for her to come closer so I could whisper to her...

"I promised him a threesome with my best friend..." She opened her mouth wide and covered it with her hand. I waved good bye and went to get in the car with Dante.

"What was that about?" Dante asked as he opened the door for us to go inside the room...

"Carol told her I was a lucky woman because you loved me and forgave me for cheating on you..." I laughed...

"I thought your information was supposed to be confidential?!"

"I know – right!" I laughed...

"So that was it?"

"Well – first she asked me where I found you..."

"Ooohhh..."

"Then she asked me how I got you to forgive me..."

"WHAT?!" he laughed...

"Yea..." I laughed...

"What'd you tell her?"

"I told her I promised you a threesome with my best friend!" I exclaimed as we both bust out laughing...

"Come sit with me..." he said as he sat down on the chaise lounge...

"I can't – I have something I need to do..."

"Why is it every time – you know what – never mind – go 'head..." he sighed. I sat down in front of the laptop, typed in connecticutonlinedivorce.com, and began to fill in the information. Dante got up to see what I was doing and then he went to lie on the bed. I closed the lap top as he picked up the remote...

"I need to go see William..."

"Why?"

"I'm going to tell him I'm getting the abortion..."

"You don't need to do that..."

"Yes I do..."

"You don't owe him anything..."

"I'm still his wife..."

"I'll be glad when this is over..."

"I'll see you when I get back..." I said on my way out...

"Does Dante know you're here?"

"Yes..." I answered as I sat down on the couch. William sat down next to me...

"Why are you here?"

"I filed for divorce..."

"You didn't come here to tell me that..."

"I need to tell you something..." I whispered as I teared up...

"Demi..." he whispered as he touched my hand...

"It's my fault..." I said as I started crying...

"No Demi – it's not your fault..."

"William... please... let me..."

"No..." he breathed as he kissed me...

"William – stop..."

"Is that what you really want?"

"I need to tell you this..."

"Okay..."

"After I moved Billy's room downstairs, he got depressed..."

"He missed being upstairs – that was normal..."

"No William – it was more than that..."

"What makes you think that?"

"Remember when Dawn took him for the weekend?"

"Yes..."

"He told Dante he wanted his room back upstairs..."

"That doesn't mean it was your fault..."

"He told Dante I moved his room downstairs because I was mad at his mother..."

"You never told him that..."

"It doesn't matter – he knew..."

"I'm sorry Demi..."

"He told Dante he wished he lived with them..."

"He said that? Why?"

"He said if he lived with them we wouldn't be fighting... and... his room wouldn't be downstairs!" I cried...

"Demi... no... It's not your fault... please... don't cry..." he whispered as he kissed me. I should've stopped him but I didn't. I needed him to forgive me and I was consumed with guilt. He pushed me back on the couch and continued kissing me... "I know you still love me..."

"Yes..."

"I knew you'd come back to me..."

"I'm not coming back to you..."

"You want me... don't deny what's happening between us..." he breathed as he moved his hands underneath my blouse...

"William... Don't..."

"Don't stop... I won't..." he breathed as he pushed his tongue in my mouth... "Mmmph... Mmmph... Mmmph..."

"Mmm... Mmm... Mmm... Mmm..." He moved his hands down my body and when he got to my pants, he hesitated before he continued... "Tell me you want me..."

"I want you..." he pushed my pants down off my legs and I heard his zipper open...

"Tell me you want me..."

"I want you..." he eased himself inside me and pushed his tongue in my mouth again as he began thrusting...

"Mmmph...   Mmmph...   Mmmph... Mmmph..."

"Mmm... Mmm... Mmm... Mmm..."

"Mmmph...   Mmmph...   Mmmph... Mmmph..."

"Mmm... Mmm... Mmm... Mmm..."

"MMMPH!   MMMPH!   MMMPH! MMMPH!"

"MMM! MMM! MMM! MMM!"

"This won't happen again..." I sighed...

"Yes it will... we belong together..."

"William – get up – I need to get dressed. He got up off me and I got dressed. I sat back down next to him and then I spoke... "That night... in the hospital..."

"We don't have to talk about that..."

"I was coming back to you..."

"You were?"

"Yes..."

"After everything I did to you – after everything I put you through – you were still coming back to me?"

"Yes..."

"Oh Demi..." he breathed as he kissed me "We can work this out – we can start over – I can change..."

"I thought so too – until Dante told me he had a vasectomy two years ago..."

"So you knew Dawn was pregnant by me before you came to see me..."

"Yes..."

"You're having my child – we can make this work – please – I know you still love me..."

"Yes William – I still love you – but I'm done with this polyamory marriage – and even if I were crazy enough to have a child with you and Dawn – Dante gave me an ultimatum..."

"An ultimatum?!"

"When I told Dante I was pregnant he told me he wouldn't help me raise your child..."

"So you're having an abortion?!"

"Yes..."

"Please – Don't kill my daughter – I'm begging you!" he cried as he got down on his knees. I started crying with him...

"I'll think about it..."

"You will?! You promise?!"

"Yes William – I promise..."

"Oh thank God! I love you!" he exclaimed as he got up off his knees and kissed me hard...

"I love you too – I need to go – we'll talk later..." I said as I went towards the door, opened it, and left...

"She's been gone for over an hour – I should've stopped her from going over there – oh God – please let her come back to me..."

"She's on her way..."

"Hey..." Dante smiled as I came in... "How'd everything go?"

"I need to tell you something..."

"I'm done..." he said as he got up...

"Dante – please – wait..."

"I'M NOT GOING TO BE THE OTHER MAN IN YOUR MARRIAGE!"

"I told him I filed for divorce..."

"You did?"

"Yes..."

"Okay – I'm listening..." he said as he sat back down...

"I needed to tell him what happened..."

"What do you mean?"

"I told him it was my fault..."

"Demi..."

"I told him everything you told me – everything Billy said – Billy was depressed – I didn't listen..." I said as I started crying...

"No you're not – stop it – it's not your fault – you hear me?"

"I couldn't help it – I started crying – he started to comfort me..."

"YOU FUCKED HIM?!"

"I didn't mean to – I swear – it just happened...

"It didn't just happen – he just happened – he saw you were vulnerable – he knows you still love him – he took advantage of you..."

"It wasn't like that Dante..."

"It was exactly like that – but anyway – you fucked him – what happened after that?"

"I told him I was going back to him..."

"IF THAT'S WHAT YOU WANT – GO!"

"I DON'T WANT THAT!"

"YOU JUST TOLD ME..."

"I told him I was going back to him that night at the hospital..."

"Oh..."

"But then you told me you had a vasectomy two years ago..."

"Okay..."

"He begged me to give him another chance..."

"Of course he did!"

"I told him I was done..."

"How many times are you going to lie to yourself?"

"I told him even if I were crazy enough to have a baby with him and Dawn – you gave me an ultimatum..."

"What did he say?"

"He got down on his knees and begged me not to kill his daughter!" I cried...

"So you've changed your mind..." he sighed. I went to stand in front of the full length mirror, opened my pants, and lifted my shirt...

"I'm sorry Demi..." I whispered as I rubbed my stomach and started crying.... "Mommy loves you..." I went into the bathroom, put on a maxi pad, came out the bathroom, and sat on the bed next to Dante. I poured myself a glass of ginger ale, drank it, and took the mifepristone... "I'm sorry Demi..." I cried as I took the misoprostol. Dante teared up as he rubbed my back. I opened the Motrin, took out two pills, and swallowed them. I poured myself another glass of ginger ale, gulped it down, and continued crying. Dante got up, helped me into bed, got into bed behind me, spooned me, and held me while I cried myself to sleep...

"Oh God..." I cried out as I woke up cramping. I got up and went to the bathroom. The pad was filled with blood so I sat down to change it. I could feel myself bleeding into the toilet... "Oh God..." I cried out again as I rocked back and forth. That Motrin didn't do shit for my cramps. I stood up, turned around, and looked in the toilet. Thank God it wasn't what I expected. I flushed the toilet, washed my hands, and went back to bed. Dante didn't say anything. He snuggled up behind me, spooned me, and rubbed my back until I fell back to sleep...

"Mommy? Where am I? I'm scared..."

"Come to the light..." The baby followed the voice...

"Who are you? Where's Mommy?"

"Keep moving – you're almost here..." The baby moved closer to the light and Billy pulled her through...

"Who are you? Where am I?"

"I'm your brother Billy..."

"My brother?"

"Yes..."

"Where am I?"

"You're in Heaven..."

"Why am I here? Why couldn't I stay with Mommy?"

"You're here because Mommy loves you..."

"Mommy loves me?"

"Yes..."

"I don't understand..."

"Don't worry – you will – I'll make sure you understand..."

"What's my name?"

"Daddy called you Demi..."

"What do I do now?"

"You come meet everyone else..." Billy answered as he took her by the hand...

"Everyone – this is my sister, Demi..."

"Hi Demi!"

"Will I see Mommy again?"

"Yes..."

"When will I see Mommy?"

"When it's time for her to come home..."

"Demi..."

"Huh?"

"C'mon..." Dante said as he sat up. He ordered room service while I was sleeping and I could smell coffee...

"Oh wow..."

"Hungry?"

"Yes..." I answered as I got out of bed...

"After we eat breakfast, we'll take a shower, get dressed, and check out..." I nodded in agreement as I sipped my coffee.

I was feeling a lot better. Dante brought all my things in from the car and we took everything into the bedroom. I filled up the walk-in closet and sighed... "I love it..."

"Me too..." We went into the guest room and put a few things in the closet. Dante moved the dresser into our bedroom, moved the bed out, and replaced it with a desk for me. I saw my computer and printer set up and I teared up... "What's wrong? You don't like it?"

"I like it... I just..."

"You miss Billy..."

"Yea..."

"I miss him too..." he sighed as he came over to me and hugged me from behind...

"Thank you..."

"You're welcome..." he said as picked up my phone and turned it on. I saw William sent me a text and when I opened it, I burst into tears...

"What's wrong?" I handed him the phone and he read Billy's obituary... "That was nice to include you..." I nodded my head as I sniffed...

"You wanna go?"

"I have – I mean – Yes – I wanna go – I need to say good bye..."

"I'm going with you..."

"Are you sure?'

"I'm going with you..."

"Okay..."

"Dante handed me back my phone and I responded to William's text...

"Thank you – we'll be there..."
"Who's we?"
"Me and Dante – is that a problem?"'
"No."

I sat down at my new desk and turned on the computer. I didn't have any new emails but I did have an email from my supervisor asking me for information about Billy... "Dante... they're doing a collection for me at work..." I sighed...

"That's nice..."

"I think I'll take the money I collect and make a donation to the Teen Empowering Network..."

"Teen Empowering Network?"

"Yes – it's a non-profit in Brunswick, GA – they empower teens, toddlers, and babies in foster care..."

"That's nice – don't they have non-profits you can donate to locally?"

"The non-profits here are bigger – they get funding all the time – I want to support this one because it's smaller – I want to help them grow..."

"Billy would like that..." I smiled, responded to my supervisor's email, and shut down the computer... "That was quick..."

"I'll look at the other emails later..." I sighed as I got up...

"What would you like to do for the rest of the day?"

"I'm not sure..." I sighed...

"I have an idea..." he whispered in my ear...

"Dante..."

"Yes..." he breathed as he began kissing my neck...

"No..."

"We need to talk..." he sighed as he took me by the hand and we went to sit down in the kitchen. I sat down at the table and he sat across from me... "Do you still love me?"

"Of course..."

"Say it..."

"It..." I said as I smiled. Dante smiled at me for a moment and then he got serious...

"You asked me to marry you..."

"Yes I did..."

"Do you still wanna get married?"

"Yes Dante..." I sighed... "I just need to process everything..."

"How much time do you think you'll need?"

"I don't know..."

"I don't think you should go to Billy's funeral..."

"I have... I have to go..."

"That's what I'm afraid of..."

"What do you mean?"

"You're already pulling away from me..."

"Dante... I'm not pulling away from you... I just..."

"You won't even let me comfort you..."

"This is because I said no..."

"If you're saying no now... what's going to happen after the funeral?"

"I'm sorry Dante – I can't help it – I loved him..."

"Are you talking about Billy? Or are you talking about William?"

"Honestly?"

"I already know the answer..." he sighed...

"I'm sorry..."

"Stop apologizing..."

"I don't know what else I can do..."

"Let me ask you something..."

"Okay..."

"If I told you I was willing to help you raise the baby..."

"No..." I interrupted...

"You didn't let me finish..."

"I don't need to let you finish – the answer is no..."

"Okay – how about this – after the funeral – before you go back to work – how about we go away for the weekend?"

"I don't know..."

"That's what worries me..."

"I'm here – with you – I chose you..."

"You're here physically – but your mind is elsewhere..."

"Yes – I have a lot on my mind – but my heart is here..." Dante got up, came over to me, pulled me up into a kiss, took my hand, and led me into the bedroom...

We spent the rest of the week getting re-acquainted. Dante went to work during the day so I had plenty of time to myself and I was grateful for the peace and quiet. I enjoyed making coffee and sitting in the office on my computer. Dante had no idea I cried for two days as it took a couple of days for me to adjust to the fact that I didn't have to get Billy ready for school and drop him off but at the same time, now that I no longer had to do it, I was realizing how much of myself I was giving and I started to feel relieved. I should've let Dawn pick him up in the morning and drop him off but hindsight is twenty-twenty and would'a-could'a-should'a doesn't do anybody any good. The good thing was that Dante wasn't pressuring me to make love and I was beginning to realize that it wasn't my fault that Billy committed suicide. I was still grieving but I didn't feel guilty anymore.

It was Friday morning. "Good morning..." he breathed as he kissed me awake...

"Good morning..." I sighed. Dante tried to comfort me but it didn't work... "I'm not ready for this..."

"Nobody's ever ready..." We both got dressed, got in the car, and went to the church. When we got there, I saw William and Dawn hugging and crying as Dante parked the car. We both got out and Dante spoke first... "I'm so sorry Dawn..."

"Thank you Dante..." William and I looked at each other and I ran to him. We hugged each other I began to sob...

"I'm so sorry..." William attempted to comfort me but Dante put a stop to it...

"Demi..." he sighed as he rubbed my back. I turned to him and he led me inside...

"I'll sit back here..." I said as I sat down. Dante sat beside me and Dawn walked past us. William came in behind her and stopped...

"Something wrong?" Dante asked...

"You shouldn't be sitting there..."

"You want us to leave?'

"Please - come sit in the front..." Dante looked at me for approval. I nodded, we both got up, and we sat in the front to the right. I could see Billy's face from where I was sitting. Dante put his arm around me and held me as I continued crying. Dawn was crying along with

William to the left. I stood up and went over to the casket...

"I'm so sorry Billy – Mommy didn't mean to make you sad – I love you..." I bent over to kiss his cheek and when I stood up, Dante was there to catch me... "C'mon – I'll get you some water..." I sat back down and Dawn was up at the casket standing with William. They were both holding each other and crying... "Here..." I took the water from him and drank it... "Are you okay?" he whispered...

"Thank God you're here..." I sighed as I took his hand. Dawn and William sat back down and the service began. I sat there but I wasn't paying attention to what was being said. When the service was over and everyone came up to say they're final good byes, Ms. Anderson sat down next to us...

"I'm so sorry for you loss..."

"Thank you..." we both said...

"We're all going to miss Billy – he was a good kid..."

"Yes he was..." Dawn said as she sat down...

"Hello Miss Taylor – I'm sorry for your loss..."

"Thank you..."

"Thank you for coming Miss Anderson..." I said as I hugged her...

"You're welcome..."

"Dante – I'm going to say good bye and then we can go..."

"Okay..." I got up and went over to William...

"I'm going to go now..."

"Thank you for coming..." he said as he pulled me into a hug..."

"I love you Billy..." I said as I touched his face...

"He loved you too..."

"Good bye Dawn..."

"Good bye..."

"Good bye Dawn..." Dante said. Dawn turned her back to him...

"C'mon Dante..." I said as I took his hand. When we got back home, I fell on the couch and sobbed. Dante sat on the couch, pulled me into his arms, and held me as I sobbed. I cried so much I gave myself a headache... "My head hurts..."

"You need to eat before you take something..."

"I'm not hungry..."

"Please – let me make you something to eat..."

"Okay..." Dante got up, took my hand, and led me back to the kitchen. I sat down and watched him take a loaf of Italian bread out the fridge. I smiled when I saw him take out honey-roasted turkey, provolone cheese, mayonnaise, lettuce, tomato, and bacon. Dante turned to look at me and smiled when he caught me smiling. After he made the sandwich, he cut it in four pieces, put them on a plate, sat it on the table, opened the fridge, and took out the ginger ale...

"Dante?"

"Yes Demi?"

"Can we get a new bed?"

"Sure..." he answered as he smiled at me mischievously.

Epilogue

*I*t was now June. Dante and I were newlyweds. William remarried Dawn. I was waiting for the I97 to meet Dante in White Plains when she called me... "Demi!" I turned around and Dawn was coming towards me...

"What the fuck does she want?' I thought to myself...

"How are you?"

"I'm good Dawn — how are you?" I asked as I looked down at her stomach...

"The baby is due in August..."

"Congratulations..."

"Thank you..."

"You don't have to thank me..."

"Yes I do..."

"For what?'

"If you didn't give William a divorce — we wouldn't've gotten a second chance..." Hearing her say that brought everything back and something in me snapped...

"I guess God works in mysterious ways..." I said as I saw the bus approaching...

"He sure does..." she sighed as the bus made a sharp turn and wound up on the curb. The driver hit the brakes but we didn't get out of the way in time...

"AAAHHH!"

"OH MY GOD – SOMEBODY CALL 911!" I screamed. Dawn was laying on the ground in front of the bus, bleeding from the waist down...

"Demi..."

"Don't talk..." I said as I bent down to hold her hand. The ambulance was first to arrive on the scene...

"Who are you?" the paramedic asked...

"Her name is Dawn Taylor – she's seven months pregnant – my name is Demi – I'll call her husband..." I answered as I took out my phone...

"Demi?"

"William – Dawn's been in an accident – she's on her way to Stamford Hospital..."

"I'm on my way..."

"William is on his way Demi..." I said as I put my phone away. The paramedics put Dawn in the ambulance and they sped off...

"Hey..."

"Dante..."

"Demi – what's wrong?!"

"It's Dawn..."

"Dawn?"

"I was waiting for the bus... she saw me... we started talking... the bus turned the corner... we didn't get out of the way fast enough..."

"ARE YOU OKAY?!"

"I'm okay... but Dawn..."

"SHE GOT HIT?!"

"Yes..."

"Is she alive?"

"I called William..."

"Where is she?"

"She went to Stamford Hospital..."

"Do you need me to come get you?"

"No – the police have some questions – I'll talk to them and then I'll come see you..."

"Where are you?"

"I'm at the Stamford Station..."

"In the Tunnel?"

"Yes..."

"I'm coming to get you..."

"Hello – can I..."

"Where's my wife?"

"Did she come by ambulance?"

"YES!"

"She in surgery..."

"Surgery?"

"Your wife was in bad shape when she got here – she lost a lot of blood..."

"Is her husband here?" the doctor asked as he walked up on them...

"I'm William Taylor – how's my wife?"

"Your wife is fine..."

"And the baby?"

"I'm sorry – we did everything we could..."

"NNNOOO!!!"

"No... I wanna stay with Mommy!"

"It's time for you to come to the light..."

"I'm scared! I want Mommy!"

"You don't have to be afraid! I promise! Come to the light!" Billy exclaimed...

"I don't wanna go..."

"You'll be okay – we promise – we love you!"

"You promise?"

"Yes – come on!" The baby went towards the light and Billy pulled her through it... "Dawn!" he exclaimed as he hugged her...

"Where am I?"

"You're in Heaven..."

"Why can't I be with Mommy?"

"Because it was time for you to come home..."

"This is home?"

"Yes..."

"Who are you?"

"I'm your brother Billy, and this is your sister Demi..."

"Hi Dawn..." Demi sighed as she gave Dawn a hug...

"How'd you know my name?'

"We heard Mommy and Daddy call you Dawn..."

"Will I see them again?"

"Yes..."

"When?"

"You can see them right now if you want..."

"I can?!"

"Yes – we watch over them..."

"I wanna see them!"

"Okay – c'mon!" Demi exclaimed as she took Dawn by the hand and pulled her towards the clouds... "Everyone – this is our sister Dawn..."

"Hi Dawn!" they all greeted...

"Why is Mommy crying?"

"She's crying because she misses you..."

"I don't want Mommy to cry..."

"We'll keep watching over them – they'll cry for a little while – and then they'll stop crying..." Billy said...

"Will we see them again?"

"Yes – when it's time for them to come home – they'll come here..." Billy answered...

"C'mon Dawn – I wanna show you the clouds!" Demi exclaimed as she took Dawn by the hand and pulled her towards the clouds...

This was the first time Dawn was back in the house in a week. She stayed in the hospital for a week due to her injuries... "I miss them so much..." she whispered as she started crying. William didn't answer her... "Where are you going?"

"I'm going upstairs..."

"I'll come with you..."

"Stay here – I'll be back in a minute..." he answered as he went into the bedroom, closed the door, and locked it. He went over to the nightstand, opened the drawer, pulled out his 38, sat down on the bed, put the gun to his head, and pulled the trigger...

"WILLIAM! NNNOOO!"

"911 – What's your emergency?"

"IT'S MY HUSBAND!" she screamed as she dropped her phone and ran upstairs...

"Daddy – c'mon!" Billy called out...

"I'm coming Billy!" William followed his voice until he got closer...

"Daddy! I can see you!"

"I see you too Billy! I'm coming!" he exclaimed as he went through the light...

"DADDY!" they all exclaimed. Billy ran to William and hugged him with Demi and Dawn right behind him...

"My babies – Billy – I missed you so much!"

"I missed you to Daddy – this is..."

"Demi!" he cried as he picked her up...

"Hi Daddy – I'm..."

"Dawn!" he cried as he bent down to pick her up with one arm while holding Demi in his other arm...

"We've been waiting for you Daddy!" Dawn exclaimed...

"You have?"

"Yes Daddy..." Billy answered... "C'mon – I'll introduce you..." he said as he motioned for

William to follow him. William smiled proudly as he followed behind Billy holding his daughters in his arms... "Everyone – this is Daddy..."

"Hi Daddy!" they all exclaimed.

DISCUSSION

1. Who do you think is responsible for Billy's suicide?

2. What would you have done in my situation?

3. Would you have had the baby?

4. Would you have beat Dawn's ass?

5. Would you be willing to be a sister wife in a polyamory marriage you didn't sign up for?

6. Do you think I pushed Dawn in front of the bus?

7. Would you have pushed Dawn in front of the bus?

8. Do you think William is a coward for committing suicide or do you understand he was overcome with grief due to losing his children?

NOTE FROM THE AUTHOR

Word-of-mouth is crucial for any author to succeed. If you enjoyed HIS WORST NIGHTMARE, please leave a review online anywhere you are able – even if it's just a sentence or two. It would make all the difference and would be very much appreciated.

Thank you.

Tracy Wilson